THE NANNY CLAUSE

KAREN ROSE SMITH

MILLS & BOON

First Published in Great Britain 2019
by Mills & Boon, an imprint of HarperCollins*Publishers*
1 London Bridge Street, London, SE1 9GF

The Nanny Clause © 2019 Harlequin Books S.A.

Special thanks and acknowledgement are given to Karen Rose Smith for her contribution to the Furever Yours series.

ISBN: 978-0-263-27231-4

0419

MIX
Paper from
responsible sources
FSC™ C007454

FSC
www.fsc.org

This book is produced from independently certified FSC™ paper to ensure responsible forest management.

For more information visit: www.harpercollins.co.uk/green

Printed and bound in Spain
by CPI, Barcelona

To my dad, who brought me my first pet.

Chapter One

Daniel Sutton studied the stack of file folders on his desk. Since he was the only lawyer in Spring Forest now, he hardly had time to schedule all of his appointments, let alone interview prospective nannies.

If only his wife and his law partner hadn't run off together. It had been over two years and that amount of time certainly should have settled any regrets he had.

Raina Clark, his secretary, knocked softly on his office door and then opened it. Raina kept his schedule on track. A widow in her late thirties, she was a good role model for his girls. She was always pleasant even when he added to her workload.

In the doorway, she announced, "Your daughters are here."

The next second Paris, Penny and Pippa burst into his office. Even his oldest, Paris, who was hitting puberty and was usually moody and sullen, seemed to be bubbling with excitement. Since he was standing, she made a beeline for his office chair and swung herself around into it. Her dark brown ponytail swayed across her shoulder.

Penny, his middle daughter who hated school and loved softball and soccer, announced with her arms spread out before her, "We're done, Dad! We're done. School's over for three whole months and I can go outside as much as I want."

Penny's light brown hair was always disheveled when she wasn't wearing her baseball cap. Yes, their private school was over for the summer, but he would have to remind Penny that she would have to choose a summer camp to keep her occupied during the day.

His youngest, Pippa, ran to him with her blond pigtails flying and wrapped her arms around his legs. "Can you come home now, Daddy, can you?"

Pippa had finally stopped crying herself to sleep at night, but she still needed a night-light. Their mother's abandonment had affected his sweet girls in so many different ways. He had to start interviews to find another compassionate nanny/housekeeper who was willing to deal with all of them. It was hard to hire a nanny who could keep up with his daughters.

In the meantime, he was becoming an expert at negotiation and compromise with his kids. They were all staring at him, waiting to see if he would leave work for them. He wished the decision was that easy.

Since all three were focused on him, he had their attention. That was rare. "How about if you give me five minutes to make a call before we go home?" Immediately he could see the disappointment on their faces so he added, "You can hang out with Raina or go outside to the yard."

The choice was easy for Penny. "Let's go to the yard. Come on."

A door at the back of the offices led outside. Penny opened it and ran down the three steps. Pippa quickly followed her. Paris begrudgingly went along.

As Daniel made the call and waited for his client to come on the line, he considered Paris and her sullenness. She was eleven. Were hormones her problem? He certainly hoped not. And Penny, at nine…when would her tomboy days end? Or would they? And darling Pippa, at seven, just seemed lost sometimes. He never thought he was doing enough. He felt he had to be a mom *and* a dad, whether he liked it or not. Sometimes that just didn't work.

Fifteen minutes later, he was ending his call when Penny rushed in. "Dad, you have to come. You have to come right now."

He jumped to his feet and ran to the door. "Has someone gotten hurt?"

"No, but come on." She took his hand and dragged him outside and around the side of the porch of the craftsman-style house where his offices occupied the first floor. On a side street, he was a short distance from everything in the historic district of Spring Forest. His daughters—even Paris—were on their knees trying to stretch inside the broken latticework surrounding the porch.

"What are you doing?" he asked, his voice louder than he intended. If there was a raccoon or something worse under there—

"It's a cat," Paris said with a little more excitement than he'd heard in her voice in a long time.

"She's a calico, Dad. She must be scared because she ran under there," Penny added.

"Of course, she's scared," he said. "The three of you are strangers to her."

Penny looked up at him, her hair flopping over her eyes. "Really, Dad? Do you think we scare her?"

Leaning closer to him, Paris whispered, "I think she's pregnant."

"You can tell that she's pregnant?" he asked in a tone matching his daughter's.

Pippa backed out from the latticework, too. Sitting cross-legged, she rounded her arms in front of her. "She's this fat. She has to be pregnant."

So much for keeping that fact quiet. Daniel knew nothing about cats. He imagined the feline could have some disease that caused swelling in her stomach. But if she *was* pregnant...

Just what was he going to do with her if she did come out of hiding? Looking at his three daughters, who were so eagerly staring at him, hoping he'd find a solution, he remembered the animal shelter on the edge of town. He sent a check to them every year so the least they could do was take this cat. But he'd have to capture her first. If she wasn't friendly and fought him, he'd need something to confine her.

"I think I have an idea," he answered. "I'll find food in my refrigerator to tempt her out. I'm sure there's a carton in the storage room that we can poke holes into so she can breathe and we can put her in that to take her to the animal shelter."

"Furever Paws?" Penny asked.

"Yes. They're good to animals and have adoption events, so I'm sure they can find her a good home."

Pippa piped up. "We can keep her, Dad."

He quickly stomped down that idea. "No, we can't. I

know nothing about cats, especially not pregnant cats. The shelter will know how to care for her best. But the first thing you have to do is back off a little and talk to her softly, to try and lure her out."

"What should we talk about?" Penny asked.

"Just tell her you want to make sure she's all right, and we're going to take her to a place where she'll be cared for. I'll find food and that box."

So much for getting work finished today. On the other hand, he'd be spending much-needed time with his daughters before he tackled the problem of hiring a nanny.

Emma Alvarez loved volunteering at Furever Paws Animal Rescue. The problem was...she needed a real job that paid. She'd made an impulsive decision and recently relocated to North Carolina from Pennsylvania—a wrong decision. She'd come because of a man. But she'd stuck around because she liked Spring Forest and the people here. The other reason she'd stayed had to do with her pride.

Emma smiled as she passed a blue-gray wall that was decorated with framed paintings from local artists. Their subjects were all breeds of cats and dogs. She headed to the front desk for a list of the latest foster parents who were available. After removing a colorful scrunchie from her shoulder-length curly dark brown hair, she refastened her ponytail. The North Carolina humidity curled her hair until she couldn't control it. Around the shelter and working with animals, keeping it tied back seemed to be the best style.

Glancing at the desk in the front lobby, Emma noticed

the chair was vacant. Possibly the volunteer had gone into the gift shop off the lobby to help a patron.

Suddenly Emma's attention swerved toward the double-glass front doors. Three children charged through the door in front of a tall man carrying a carton. A tall *handsome* man. She diverted her attention to the holes that had been cut into the sides of the box. Emma suspected an animal was contained inside.

The newcomer, with dark brown hair cut short and neat, wearing a businesslike white oxford shirt, had a commanding presence as his deep voice advised the girls, "Slow down until we know where we're going."

His daughters, perhaps?

Emma suspected he might be a professional man, not only because of the crisp button-down shirt—though he'd rolled up the sleeves—but also because of the pressed charcoal-gray slacks he wore along with the leather loafers. She hadn't seen him here before.

Two of the girls were chattering away. The middle one, who looked about nine, wore a baseball cap backward and pulled on her dad's elbow. "What will they do with her? Where will they put her? How long will they keep her?"

The smallest child seemed to be enamored with the paintings on the walls. "Isn't that cool?" She was pointing to a photo of a cat that had been color-blocked with digital photography.

The oldest child didn't seem to be reacting to anything. Eleven or twelve, maybe, Emma guessed. All three girls were dressed in colorful skirts and blouses.

The man raised his gaze to Emma's. His eyes were green. To her dismay, she couldn't seem to look away.

Thank goodness, *he* finally did, as he moved toward

her. "Are you the person in charge?" His gaze ran down her outfit—a white T-shirt with the red logo of the shelter that was a profile of a dog and a cat in a heart—and jeans. Her wardrobe was minimal because she'd come to Spring Forest on an impulse, a very bad impulse. When she remembered that, she knew she couldn't let herself be mesmerized by a man's eyes or his words or his smile. Not ever again.

"I guess you could say I'm in charge at the moment. How can I help you?"

The three girls crossed to her. The smallest explained eagerly, "We found her at my dad's law office under the porch. We think she's pregnant."

"It's a cat," the middle child explained. "She's white with spots of black and gold and brown on her back."

"Then she must be a calico," Emma suggested.

Finally, the oldest spoke. "That's what my dad's phone said. I researched photos of cats."

The smallest one again piped up. "Paris can't have a phone 'til she's twelve, and that's only if she's ree-spon-si-ble." The little girl drew out the word as if it was very important.

"Girls, let's introduce ourselves before you overwhelm this nice lady. I'm Daniel Sutton," he said. "And these are my daughters—Paris, Penny and Pippa."

"I'm Penny," the middle child added, raising her hand.

"I'm Emma Alvarez," Emma returned.

"Who painted these pictures hanging on the walls?" the youngest one asked.

Emma smiled at the child, who looked totally interested. "They're all done by local artists. Do you like to draw?"

"Yes. But I'm not very good. I like to look at paintings."

With a smile—a smile that really did make her stomach quiver a bit—Daniel Sutton asked, "Where would you like me to take the cat? I don't know much about your facility. This is the first I've been here since the tornado hit in March."

From what Emma understood, the shelter had been renovated since the tornado. Some renovations were still in progress. "Are you sure the cat you found doesn't belong to a neighbor?" Emma asked.

"I checked with neighbors on both sides before we brought her in. They don't have cats and didn't recognize the description of this one. You are going to take her, aren't you? I've made donations over the years…"

Donations were important, Emma had to admit, but that had nothing to do with whether they took an animal or not. "I'll have to take her back to the quarantine area."

Pippa asked, "What's quarantine?"

Paris didn't give Emma time to answer. "That's a place where the animal has to stay all alone to see if she has any diseases."

"I don't want her to stay all alone," Penny said with a scowl.

"She won't exactly be all alone," Emma explained. "She's separated from the other animals so that we can make sure she's healthy. We'll scan her, too, to see if she's microchipped. If she is, that would help us find her owner."

Daniel Sutton's eyes held a myriad of questions, probably tough ones about what they'd do if the cat was seriously ill. Emma didn't want to answer them around his daughters.

"Can we go with her?" Pippa asked.

Emma crouched down to Pippa in order to make eye-to-eye contact. "I'll tell you what. Why don't you and Paris and Penny come part of the way with me. You can look through the glass wall at the other cats we have who are waiting to be adopted."

"Do you have pups, too?" Paris asked.

"We do. You can see those also. Meanwhile, I'll take this calico back to the quarantine area and I'll talk to our vet tech. She'll have to check her and see what might have to be done to care for her." Emma's gaze returned to Daniel's. "I have paperwork you'll have to fill out. If you want to wait with your daughters, I'll collect it and bring it out."

She reached for the box that the lawyer held in his hands. It looked as if it had once held reams of paper and it had handles on either side. After she took the box, she set it on a nearby table. "I just want to take a peek. I'm sure your girls probably want to wish her well, too."

Pippa, Paris and Penny all gathered around the box as Emma removed the lid. "Oh, aren't you a pretty girl," Emma said. Her white fur was a bit dirty but her colors were vibrant.

"Are you going to give her a bath?" Pippa asked.

Emma laughed. "I doubt that. When she's cared for and has enough to eat, she'll groom herself. That's what cats do. My guess is she's tired from running here and there, trying to find a place out of the weather and get something to eat."

The girls seemed to be hanging on her every word.

When Emma glanced up at Daniel Sutton, he was watching her. His expression was...*curious*, if she had to put a word to it. She was curious about him, too, but had no right to be. He was probably married.

There wasn't a ring on his finger, but she knew better

than most that the symbol of marriage might not mean anything.

Reminding herself that her only interest was the cat in front of her, and maybe the girls, she asked, "Did she give you any trouble when you handled her?"

Daniel shook his head. "She was compliant, even purred a little when Penny petted her."

"Did you give her anything to eat?"

"I had roasted chicken in my office refrigerator. I cut off a piece and chopped it up. She gobbled it down."

"Really fast," Pippa added.

Paris said quietly, "She rubbed against my legs, too, over and over again, like she wanted to be friends."

The cat was looking at Emma as if asking what was going to happen next. Emma wished she knew and hoped for the best.

Daniel felt shaken after Emma Alvarez walked away. He hadn't been attracted to a woman since Lydia had left. What *was* this?

Obviously, Emma was compassionate, not only with animals, but also with children. Before Lydia left, he hadn't even seen that compassion in his ex-wife toward her own offspring, much less strangers.

Don't compare anything. Don't be interested in any-one, he charged himself. He finally felt as if he was whole again and that had taken two long years.

The other stray thought he'd had about Emma Alvarez was that she'd make a wonderful nanny. He'd interviewed two women last week and neither of them had given him the impression they'd be this good with his girls.

Too picky…or too cautious? Both were true on many fronts. But Emma gave him a feeling he just couldn't ignore, especially as he watched his daughters respond to her. Yeah, he was definitely going with his gut on this.

He watched Emma speak with a volunteer, who was caring for the cats behind the plexiglass window. That woman asked Pippa, Penny and Paris if they wanted to come in and pet a few. They did. He watched them curiously as he waited for Emma. Paris obviously had a caring streak, too. He hadn't seen that side of her since Lydia had left.

Emma returned from the office down the hall with papers that were attached to a clipboard in hand. She said, "Why don't we sit in the lobby while you fill these out. If you have any questions, I'll be here to answer them."

Daniel gently rapped on the window and Paris looked his way. He pointed to the clipboard and to the lobby, and she gave him a thumbs-up sign to indicate that she understood.

As they walked toward the lobby, Emma said to Daniel, "The feline you brought in was not microchipped. She will have to have an FIV and a feline leukemia test. I didn't want to say anything around your girls."

"What do you mean? What if one of the tests is positive?"

Emma gave him a sad look and he knew what that meant.

"Why?" he asked, surprised that he cared.

"There's research being done to determine if an FIV-positive cat can be included in a multi-cat family, but for now FIV and feline leukemia are both considered highly contagious." She gently touched his arm.

He couldn't believe the heat that simple touch generated. When he glanced at her, he saw an almost surprised look on her face. Was she affected, too?

They'd reached the lobby and Emma cleared her throat and motioned to two chairs. After they sat, she handed him the clipboard and pen. They were sitting side by side, his knee practically touching hers. He didn't move it away because that would be too obvious. Obvious that he was attracted? Or obvious that he wanted to remove himself?

He rested the clipboard on his thigh. The realization brought on by Emma's words struck hard. "If you can't save that cat and her kittens, my daughters are going to be heartbroken."

"I do understand," Emma empathized. "And you shouldn't lose hope—the tests might come back negative. As soon as the vet tech is free, she'll draw blood. The test will take about twenty minutes. I suggest you take your daughters home and I'll call you later with the results."

He made a quick decision. "Let me give you my cell number, then you can reach me no matter where I am. Do you have your phone on you?"

She did. She plucked her phone from her belt and tapped Daniel's cell number into her contacts.

Thinking he should be filling out the forms, not watching Emma tap in his contact information, he felt startled when she raised her gaze to his and didn't quickly turn away.

He *did* look away. The forms had become more important than Emma Alvarez.

Daniel sat in his study that evening listening to his girls play a video game in the family room across the hall. The floor plan of this house was one of the reasons he and his ex-wife had bought it after Penny was born. The house had been on the market for over a year without a buyer. The owners, a couple whose family had grown and left, had wanted to move closer to their children. He'd gotten a great deal, and he knew that. Lydia had been over-the-moon pleased.

Pippa's laughter rang out from the family room. He glanced around his man cave at the bookshelves, at the massive desk, at the computer-and-printer setup. Neither his house nor his law degree would mean anything to him without his daughters.

He returned to looking for summer-camp selections for his girls at the community college. He hoped it wasn't too late to enroll. As he began reading the selections, his cell phone buzzed. Picking it up, he saw on the screen that the caller was E. Alvarez. His heart began beating just a little faster.

"Mr. Sutton?" she asked.

"Call me Daniel," he suggested. That wasn't too informal, right? He always told his clients that, didn't he?

Emma hesitated and then said, "All right, Daniel. The calico tested negative, and we're taking care of her. I named her Fiesta because of all of her colors. She needs good nutrition for her babies."

"I'm so glad she has a place where she'll be safe," Daniel responded.

"She'll be safe for a time. Momma cats with babies aren't very adoptable. The kittens will be, though, once they're born."

"I don't think I'm going to tell Pippa, Penny and Paris that."

"We can't give Fiesta a whole lot of attention at the shelter because of all of our animals. I'll do my best to keep an eye on her. It really would be better if she could go home with you and your girls, though."

"No." The word popped out of Daniel's mouth before he even thought about the idea.

"Can I ask why?" she inquired gently.

After a moment, he told her the truth. "I'm a divorced single dad with three girls who are active, smart and sometimes needy. I really can't see adding a pet to that mix."

She paused, then said quietly, "I see. If you can't adopt Fiesta, why don't you bring your daughters back to the shelter for a visit. I'm sure they'd enjoy it and so would she. I'm certain she'll want all the attention she can get. She's a very friendly feline."

"I'll consider a visit," he assured her, maybe because he wanted to see Emma Alvarez again and not the cat.

"Whenever you have time. Do you know our hours?"

"I do. I looked them up before we came to the shelter. Are you always on the same shift?"

"My schedule varies depending on when the shelter needs me to be here."

He hadn't thought about that.

"We hope to see you soon at Furever Paws," she said politely. "You have a good night and say hello to your girls for me."

"I will."

After Daniel ended the call, he wished it had gone on a little longer. Should he visit again with her at Furever Paws when he was attracted to her?

His better judgment told him *no*.

Chapter Two

Whole Bean, the coffee shop in Spring Forest, was a popular local gathering place, even on a Saturday. Daniel was grateful for his sister, who had come over to the house to take care of the girls for the day so he could catch up on client appointments at the office. She was making them breakfast and since she didn't drink coffee…

The coffee shop was near his office so it was an easy stop. He went to the counter and ordered a double-shot espresso. Checking his watch, he saw that he had about ten minutes before he wanted to start at the office. It wouldn't hurt to relax a bit before the workday began. Sometimes getting the girls up and dressed and their hair fixed was like running a marathon. He wanted his sister to do the fun things with them and didn't intend to burden her with any more than was necessary.

He'd turned and headed to the main part of the café to find a table when he stopped cold. There was Emma

Alvarez, sitting alone at a bistro table for two. Could she be waiting for someone?

It didn't look like it. She'd spread the newspaper on the table in front of her and had a pen in her hand.

So much for relaxing. His heart had started pulsing faster the moment he'd spotted her.

Crossing to the table, he stood there for a moment. She must have felt his presence because she looked up and her eyes widened.

Before he could stop himself, he asked, "Do you mind if I join you?"

She looked flustered but she folded the newspaper and laid her pen on the table. "I don't mind."

He checked the coffee she was drinking. It looked like a latte.

She saw him studying her coffee and she studied his. "Yes, I drink lattes—vanilla. How about you?"

He nodded to his cup as he sat. "It only looks like black coffee. It has shots of espresso in it."

"Enough to get you through the day?" she teased. "Or will you need more about noon?"

"I'm limiting myself to the two shots of espresso a day. If I have them both in the morning, that's it. I have enough trouble sleeping at night."

"Because of your daughters?" she asked, and then blushed. "I'm sorry. That sounded like prying."

"I opened the conversation, and yes, my daughters do keep me from sleeping at night. Pippa often calls out in her sleep. It's been that way since my wife left."

"You said you're divorced?"

His gaze landed on her hand. No ring there. "Yes, I'm divorced. Two years now. You'd think I would have gotten used to being mother and father by now."

Emma shook her head. "I don't think it works that way. I lost my mom to cancer when I was twelve. I'll never forget those last six months or the years after, when I missed her so much I didn't know what to do. I still miss her."

They'd jumped into heavy waters awfully fast, and it was time to back up. Except, when he tried to remove himself emotionally, he got caught up in Emma's beauty—those dangling curls, her pert nose, her full lips. Backing away from her would be downright difficult.

Clearing his throat, he nodded to the newspaper. "You looked serious when I came over."

"I'm looking for a job. I have a business degree. In Pennsylvania before I moved here, I was an office manager. I'm hoping that the grapevine surrounding the shelter will reveal a position somewhere nearby. Lots of folks go in and out of there in a day."

"I imagine so. I thought maybe you were training to be a vet tech since you were working at the shelter."

"Oh, I love animals. But I don't think vet tech is in my future—the medical side isn't for me. During my shift I help out wherever's necessary. What I like most is giving the animals attention. They are so much like children. When neglected, they act out. If we play with them to release energy, and they know someone's caring for them, they behave much better."

When he was at the shelter with his daughters, he could easily see that Emma had a soft spot for children *and* animals. He took a few sips of his coffee. "Have you been in North Carolina long?"

"About a month now."

"You said you worked as an office manager in Pennsylvania. Did you come here looking for work?"

Appearing uncomfortable for a moment, she brushed

her curls behind her ear before answering him. "Not exactly. It's a very long story. My trip down here ended up being a little different than I expected. Now I've decided to stay for a while to see if Spring Forest is where I might want to settle. It is a beautiful little town."

Emma sipped more of her coffee. It was about half-finished. It must have still had foam because it edged her upper lip. He smiled.

"What?" she asked, probably because he was studying her so intently.

What he wanted to do was touch that foam and find out exactly how soft her skin was. The notion was absolutely crazy. So instead he took his forefinger and edged his own upper lip.

She laughed and caught on right away. "You don't have to worry about that with espresso."

She wasn't at all embarrassed and he liked that about her. She was natural, unaffected, genuine.

The lawyer in him took the other side of the argument. *You don't know her. You have barely spent any time with her. How could you possibly know she's all those things?*

Yes, how could he possibly know, and why would he want to know? He had a full plate as it was. He didn't need an entanglement to upset an already rocky boat.

Although he was reluctant to leave, he made a point of checking his watch. Then he said, "I hope you find what you're looking for. I really need to go now. I have a client coming in first thing this morning."

She nodded, "I understand. You have a good day."

He stood, even though something was telling him to stay. He waved his hand at her coffee cup. "Enjoy the rest of your latte."

She was smiling at him when he left. That smile stayed with him all the way to his office.

Tied up with clients who wanted to make out a will, close on a house sale or draw up powers of attorney, Daniel hardly had time to breathe the rest of the morning. At some point the espresso would let him down, but hopefully not until the end of the afternoon. Raina knew he liked to see clients in the morning and deal with paperwork later in the day.

He'd started reading the history of a neighborly dispute over land boundaries between two properties when his cell phone buzzed. Cell phone rather than office phone meant it was a personal call.

"Hello," he said. "Busy lawyer here."

"Oh, Dad, you're always busy," Paris complained. "I have a problem. Aunt Shannon wants me to eat a sandwich *and* a salad. I don't want to. She's so vehement about it, I'm afraid she'll force-feed me."

Just where had Paris learned the word *vehement*? She wasn't studying for her SATs yet, he thought wryly. However, when Paris was in a snit he did his best to calm her. "Do you want me to talk to your aunt? You can put her on the phone."

"No. You have to come home. I've got to lose weight before school starts in September. She doesn't understand that. Oh, and Penny missed her last soccer game of the season this morning because you didn't tell Aunt Shannon about it."

Daniel rubbed his hand over his brow. "Why didn't Penny tell her about it?"

He could almost hear the shrug in Paris's voice when

she answered, "I guess she forgot, too. It was scheduled at the last minute."

He had a decision to make—whether to be honest or patronizing. Paris didn't take patronizing well. "I do have to work. Are you sure you can't settle this yourself?"

"I didn't tell you the worst part."

Now Daniel held in a breath, then let it out. "The worst part?"

"Um…" Paris hesitated. That was unusual and worried Daniel even more.

"Just spill it, Paris. It won't get any easier if you turn it around in your mind ten times."

"Pippa got into something you're not going to like."

"Is this going to be twenty questions?" He really was losing patience. Maybe he should take up meditation.

"There was this shoebox in your closet. It had all of mom's makeup in it. Now it's all over Pippa's face."

Pushing aside the papers on his desk, Daniel faced the problem head-on. When Lydia had left, he'd hoped she'd return to her family, so he'd kept all of her things. When she hadn't, he'd packed everything up and then forgotten about that box in the deepest recesses of his closet.

"What made Pippa go in there in the first place?" he asked Paris.

"I don't know. Honest. Maybe she saw you put it in there and she remembered."

More than once Pippa had asked why her mommy had left. He'd never been exactly sure what to tell her. Lydia sent the girls birthday cards and she'd written them a couple of short notes, but that had been the extent of her communication since the divorce. No wonder they felt abandoned.

What had Emma said just this morning? *Animals are so much like children. When neglected, they act out.*

So much for working at his office on a Saturday. "I'll be home in about ten minutes, Paris. Do you think the three of you would like to visit Fiesta at Furever Paws?"

"Dad's coming home," Paris announced to her sisters, who must have been standing right there.

He heard the "yay" that filled the kitchen. Then Paris asked Pippa and Penny, "Do you want to go visit Fiesta at Furever Paws?"

Their yeses were loud and clear. So were their needs. Shannon was great with them but they needed somebody full-time who concentrated just on them. They needed a nanny.

An idea zipped through his mind. Emma needed a job. Maybe she'd consider coming to work for him as a nanny. However, he wouldn't hire her on a whim. He needed to speak to Rebekah Taylor, the shelter director, to see what Emma was like as a volunteer. This visit to Fiesta could suit more than one purpose.

Emma saw them coming. She had just finished the paperwork and handed over the cutest black toy poodle to his adoptive parents. The woman, who was about sixty, stood back until Daniel's daughters entered, then Daniel waited for her to leave with her dog.

When Penny and Pippa spotted Emma, they ran right over to her. Paris proceeded more slowly. Pippa looked up at her with her big chocolate-brown eyes. "We came to see Fiesta. Can she have visitors?"

Emma smiled. "Sure, she can have visitors. We gave her a special little home with her own litter box and a plastic bin with shredded newspaper that she can use when she feels her babies are going to be born."

Now Paris gave her attention to Emma, too. "Why shredded newspaper?"

"Because it can be replaced easily. Cats also like to lie in paper for some reason."

Daniel eyed Emma, and when he did, she felt herself blush. What was it about this man that made him so attractive? Sure, he was tall. He was handsome. He cared about his daughters and an animal he'd found under his porch, too. But none of that proved he'd be a good romantic prospect.

No more impulsive decisions, Emma told herself fiercely. Her last impulsive decision had landed her here in Spring Forest without a job or a place to stay. Living in a studio apartment with a month-to-month lease, she'd used up most of her savings. She needed to find a job fast…that is if she was going to stay in Spring Forest.

If she didn't find a job soon that paid her a decent wage, she'd *have* to return home. She really didn't want to do that because it would prove her father had been right.

She motioned the girls down the hall. "Turn left at the first door."

Daniel walked beside her and she was totally aware of him. His navy striped tie was tugged down and the top two buttons of his royal blue oxford shirt were open. Suddenly he touched her elbow and they both paused. Her arm felt as if he'd touched her with fire.

"You must be a miracle worker," he said.

She felt stunned by his touch and immobilized by the admiration in his eyes. Somehow she found her voice. "Why do you say that?"

"Because Paris doesn't talk to anyone unless she has

to. And she never asks questions. She acts as if she knows everything about everything. With you, she's different."

"I'm just a new person in her life. I love animals, and maybe she does, too."

Daniel was still looking at her as if he was debating something in his mind. Finally he said, "You're good with Penny and Pippa, too. Pippa has had a hard time. She'd rather I hug her and keep her with me rather than doing anything else."

"Daddy's little girl?" Emma asked, knowingly.

"Maybe. Or maybe she's just holding on to her only remaining parent for dear life. I don't know if you noticed, but she still has the stain of lipstick under her nose."

"Lipstick?" Emma asked, confused.

"When I got home today, she'd gotten into Lydia's old stuff that I'd dumped into a shoebox and stored in my closet. She had a thick coat of lipstick all around her mouth, eye shadow on her eyes, blush on her cheeks, and she looked like a clown."

"You didn't laugh, did you?" Little girls usually looked to their dad for affirmation as well as attention.

"No. I was too disconcerted to do that. But I didn't tell her she looked beautiful, either."

"What did you tell her?" She knew whatever Daniel had told his daughter would stick.

"I told her she was much prettier with nothing at all on her face."

Emma couldn't help but smile. "You're a very smart dad."

"Penny doesn't think so. We both forgot about her soccer game."

Emma tried hard not to widen her smile at his adorably sheepish tone. He was a dad on his own, doing the best he could. "I think you're too hard on yourself."

"You don't know me," he reminded her with a frown.

"I can see you want the best for your daughters."

Again Daniel eyed her as if he was debating with himself. However, he changed the course of their conversation. "I hear the director of the shelter is Rebekah Taylor."

"Yes, Rebekah's the director."

"Do you think I could meet with her?"

"She has a board meeting this morning over at the Whitakers'." The Whitaker sisters, Bunny and Birdie, had invested their money in this shelter to set it up. Although she'd seen them around the shelter, she'd never met them officially. But she'd heard a lot about them.

"I can leave a message for Rebekah with your number. I'm sure she'll call you back."

"I'd like that. Thank you for offering."

Emma could get lost in Daniel's green eyes, but she knew she wouldn't. She absolutely wouldn't.

During the next half hour, Daniel and his daughters gave Fiesta some of the attention she deserved.

Penny marveled at her colors. "She's so pretty—white, and black, and brown. I'd never seen a cat like her."

"I wonder what color her babies will be," Paris commented.

"They could be a variety of colors," Emma explained. "It will be exciting to see them, won't it?"

Pippa came over to Emma and leaned against her leg. "Will we be able to play with the kittens?"

"I don't know, honey," Emma said. "It depends if someone adopts her before she has her babies."

Pippa leaned her head against Emma's waist. "Daddy doesn't want a cat and babies."

Emma couldn't help but put an arm around Pippa and

pat her shoulder. Then her gaze met Daniel's and she was hard-pressed to look away.

After Daniel and his daughters left, Emma couldn't forget how his touch had made her feel. She also couldn't forget how his daughters had warmed her heart. She wondered again why Daniel wanted to talk to Rebekah. She'd left his message on the director's desk. But since Rebekah had come back from the board meeting, she'd been busy around the shelter.

Emma almost ran into her as she came out of her office, cell phone in hand. She'd apparently just ended a call.

"Something important?" Emma asked.

"It was Grant Whitaker," Rebekah told her. "He just..." Rebekah shook her head. "I'll take care of it. Nothing to worry about. I saw the message you put on my desk from Daniel Sutton. He's the lawyer around here, isn't he?"

"Yes, he is. He and his daughters brought Fiesta in yesterday."

"Does he want to adopt the cat?"

"No. I don't know what he wants."

"I'll get back to him as soon as I can, but the way this day's going, that might not be until this evening."

"He said whenever you have time would be fine."

"Good. No pressure. That's what I like from a man." She sighed. "I'm going to check the work on the expansion porch for the cats. That's where I'll be if anybody needs me."

After Rebekah turned in that direction, Emma returned to Fiesta. She hadn't told Daniel and his daughters but Fiesta wasn't eating as she should. Emma hoped she just needed to become acclimated, but she'd ask the vet, Doc J, to check her again when he made his rounds tomorrow morning.

She would keep her focus on the cat, not on Daniel Sutton.

Daniel didn't like the atmosphere when he and his daughters exited Furever Paws. They were quiet—much too quiet. Maybe he *should* consider adopting Fiesta. Paris had seemed more outgoing around the cat. Penny and Pippa were obviously affectionate with her. One thing he had to be with his kids was flexible.

He could check YouTube for *cats*, *pregnancy* and *delivery*.

That evening he did just that. He'd never looked into the care of animals that much, and now he realized the extent of the volunteers' work at Furever Paws. They had to love what they were doing. In many ways it was similar to running a day care for kids.

There was a light rap on his den door. When he turned, he saw Paris. That was a surprise. She usually didn't seek him out. "What's up?" he asked nonchalantly.

"I want to keep practicing with the swim team this summer. Are you going to let me? I need the exercise and swimming is one of the best ways to get it."

He knew Paris was correct in her assessment that swimming was great exercise, but he wished she wanted to be part of the team for the sportsmanship and camaraderie. Lydia had used exercise for weight control and had become almost obsessive about it. He didn't want Paris to emulate that behavior.

"I'll consider it, but I want you to consider attending one of these educational camps this summer."

Wrinkling her nose, Paris frowned. "Are you serious? Is this a negotiation?"

He didn't know if becoming a lawyer was in the genes, but Paris sure had some of his. "I guess you could say that, or you could call it a compromise. What do you think?"

"If that's the only way I get to be on the summer swim team, okay." With that she turned and left his office.

He thought about going after her and furthering their discussion, but his landline phone rang. He scooped it up from the desk and saw the caller ID—R Taylor was calling. "Hello, Miss Taylor. I see you received my message."

"I did. How can I help you?"

"It's about Emma Alvarez."

"Yes?" she asked, prompting him.

"I'm thinking about hiring her. Would you give her a recommendation?"

"I'd give Emma five stars in everything she does. She's an enthusiastic volunteer, and she doesn't just do the work, she *feels* the work. She has a connection to the animals."

"Did she give you references?"

"Certainly. I wouldn't have taken her on if she hadn't. Even volunteers go through a background check and vetting process. Her references are stellar. If I had to sum it up, I'd say she's reliable, prompt and a problem solver, besides being patient with animals."

That was all Daniel needed to know. Those recommendations would be a perfect résumé for a nanny. "Can you tell me if she's volunteering tomorrow?"

"Actually, yes. She'll be here after ten."

Daniel knew exactly where he'd be headed after church tomorrow—to Furever Paws to find a solution to one very big problem.

Chapter Three

The next morning after church, Daniel stopped at Furever Paws with Paris, Penny and Pippa. They'd been less restless in church today because they'd known they would be coming here afterward.

After they went inside, it took a volunteer a bit of time to find Emma. They were finally told that she was in the dog room, cleaning cages. Daniel and his girls went that way.

He rapped on the window and Emma saw him. She smiled and came out.

Penny asked, "Can we go in and play with a puppy?"

"I'll let two out of their cages," Emma said. "We have beagle puppies, who are adorable." After she did that and the girls were engaged, Emma returned to Daniel. "I understand you wanted to speak with me."

"I do. I'd like somewhere more private, but I know you have to keep an eye on the girls."

"Yes, I do. If the puppies become overexcited or your daughters get too rambunctious, I'll have to step in."

Daniel had pulled a folded paper from his back pocket. He could see in Emma's eyes that she was wondering what it was. "Let me begin by saying I talked with Rebekah about you."

Emma's mouth opened and she immediately asked, "Did I do something wrong?"

"Oh, no! Nothing like that." He reached for her and clasped her elbow. "You've done everything right according to Rebekah. You're a five-star volunteer."

Emma smiled but gradually her smile slipped away. "I still don't understand why you needed to talk with her about me."

"You need a job, and I need a nanny-slash-housekeeper."

Emma studied him for a long moment, and he saw wariness in her eyes. He didn't blame her.

"Since my last nanny left, my sister Shannon has been watching the girls when I need her to. But the problem is… I'm taking advantage of her. She has a three-year-old and it's hard for her to watch her toddler and my three kids. With the girls out of school now, she's coming over to my house to watch them. She does her best, but it's too much to ask her to keep track of everything going on in my house and in hers, too. Paris called me yesterday, and I had to run home to settle a few issues. My daughters are more important to me than any work, but I have to work to sustain us all. I've interviewed people for the nanny position," he went on, "and I just can't find anyone I like."

"Why me?" Emma asked, maybe looking a bit interested now.

"Because from the first day I walked in here with

Paris, Pippa and Penny, they related to you. You're compassionate and caring and seem to be able to handle them better than I do. I know expertise when I see it."

"I've never been a nanny. I was an office manager."

"If you throw in compassion, kindness and firmness, there's not much difference between an office manager and a nanny, don't you think?"

Emma smiled at his wry tone. "I don't know, Daniel…"

He handed her the paper in his hand. "This is a list of *my* references. You can check them all."

When she still seemed hesitant, he added, "The job includes room and board. There's an in-law suite. You'd have privacy when you need it."

Emma studied the paper. "I'll check your references and I'll think about your offer. That's all I can tell you right now."

"At least you didn't say *no*, so that's progress for me." He grinned at her, hoping she'd realize he was an okay guy.

They couldn't shake on it since they hadn't made a deal yet, but he nodded. "We have a little time before we have to be at Shannon's for lunch. Maybe you could spend it with my daughters?"

With no hesitation whatsoever, Emma nodded to the dog room. "I suggest we play with the beagle puppies with the girls."

Knowing that could be a bonding experience, he opened the door to the room and let Emma precede him inside.

Standing in the cleaned-up and almost spotless kitchen on Monday, Daniel realized how happy he was

that Emma had agreed to be his daughters' nanny. She'd
called him last evening to accept his offer. Daniel was
ready for her…at least, he thought he was. The girls certainly were. Pippa and Penny were dancing all around,
chattering with excitement. Paris wasn't as noisy but she
didn't have a solemn look on her face, either.

He'd made sure there weren't any dirty dishes in the
sink. He'd made sure the great room was as straightened
up as it could be. He'd told his daughters to at least give
the room a half hour after Emma arrived before they
messed it up again.

They'd laughed. They hadn't thought he was serious.

He'd looked out the front Palladian windows for at
least the tenth time when his cell phone buzzed. Taking it
from his belt, he was concerned it was Emma telling him
she'd changed her mind. But it wasn't. It was his sister.

Without preamble, she said, "I still think you're crazy
to hire a stranger."

He could imagine Shannon's red curls flying and her
lips, which were usually turned up in a smile, pointing
downward.

"Good morning to you, too, sis."

"You should have used an agency."

"As I told you before, I tried an agency. The appli-
cants they sent never could have kept up with the girls.
You know how much energy they have."

His sister was silent until she said, "Yes, they have
energy, but they need it to be channeled in the right way.
What makes you think this woman can do that? It's not
like she was a schoolteacher or worked in day care."

"Working with animals is like working in day care,"
he muttered.

"Don't try to snow me," Shannon protested.

"I'll tell you what. I'll invite you to dinner as soon as Emma's settled in. How would that be?"

"Sooner," Shannon demanded.

"You know, you always were a bossy kid sister."

"And you were always a know-it-all older brother."

They both laughed. Thank goodness they could laugh. It kept them sane when the world turned upside down.

Suddenly he heard a car in the driveway. It was a compact blue sporty model. Just like Emma, he supposed—full of class and energy. "I gotta go. She's here."

"You can always call me if she doesn't work out."

"Bye, Shannon." He ended the call and replaced his phone on its dock.

He watched as Emma stepped out of her car. He felt his pulse race a little faster as first one bare leg appeared and then the other. As she closed the driver's-side door, his breath actually caught. She'd worn pale pink shorts—a respectable length—and a puff-sleeved gauzy white blouse. Her curly hair blew in the wind. He noticed her sandals had little jewel-like beads on them. Pippa would love that.

Emma stepped to the back door of the sedan and pulled out a messenger bag.

He told his daughters, "I'm going to help Emma bring her things in." He hurried out the front door and down the walk then took the side path to the driveway. When Emma saw him, she smiled.

That smile.

Maybe he'd made a huge mistake. He was attracted to her even more than he'd realized.

On the other hand, he needed a nanny. He'd keep that attraction in check.

"Welcome to the Sutton abode." As soon as he said it, he thought it sounded lame.

Emma didn't seem to notice. "It's good to be here. You can't imagine how thankful I am that I found a job."

"If you have other suitcases, the girls can help."

The smile left Emma's face. "One suitcase."

He knew Lydia never went anywhere, even for just a weekend, without three suitcases. This was Emma's life…in one suitcase?

His thoughts must have shown on his face. "I suppose you're wondering why I didn't bring many belongings to North Carolina."

"You travel light?" he joked.

Silence fell over them until a mower at a neighbor's house started up. Then Emma responded, "I impulsively moved to Spring Forest, intending to have other items shipped later. But since I only had a small studio apartment, that just didn't happen. I wanted to wait until I was settled somewhere."

"Is taking this position another impulsive decision on your part?" After all, he had to ask questions if he wanted to get to know her and her personality. That was important when he saw her interacting with his girls. It was the only way he'd know if this was going to work out. He had to be protective of his daughters.

"I'm not sure how impulsive it is," she said, looking directly into his eyes. "I made this decision out of necessity. I needed a job and I really didn't want to return to Pennsylvania."

When she didn't explain further, he decided to let the discussion go for now. There would be time aplenty to get to know Emma Alvarez. After all, they would both be living under the same roof.

* * *

A short time later, after Daniel reluctantly left for work, Pippa, Penny and Paris took Emma on a tour of the house. It was a large house with a covered entry in the front leading into the foyer. The room to the left, the girls explained, was Daniel's home office. It was easy to see that when Emma peeked in. Across the foyer on the right was the living room. Straight ahead Emma could see the great room with a vaulted ceiling. There was also a stairway that led upstairs.

The kitchen and the dining room were off the great room and there was a mudroom and a laundry room, as well as a bathroom.

Penny looked at her older sister, Paris, and said, "Let's show her her room."

Emma was anxious to see where she'd be staying.

The girls led her down the hall past Daniel's study and turned left. When Emma stepped inside, she realized the suite resembled a studio apartment. There was a double bed, a sitting area and a kitchenette. A full bath off the room meant she'd have complete privacy if she wanted it. When she was done for the day and came in here for the night, there was no reason for her to have to go into the rest of the house. She liked that, and already felt more comfortable about being here. The house was in order but Emma could easily see it needed a good dusting and a sweeper run over the carpet.

She asked Paris, "How long has it been since your nanny left?"

"Two weeks," Paris responded but didn't explain further.

"The first thing we need to do," Emma told them,

"is to clean. Can you show me where the cleaning supplies are?"

"I thought you were going to spend time with us," Penny complained.

"Oh, I am. You're going to help me clean."

"No way," Paris mumbled. Pippa and Penny looked as if they were going to revolt, too.

"I'll tell you what. We'll make a game of it. And your reward for helping will be a visit to Fiesta. What do you think?"

"We can really visit Fiesta?" Pippa asked.

"Sure. I'm certain she'd like the company. I'll put each chore on a slip of paper in a bowl. We'll draw them out one at a time. When we finish one, we draw another and start on that. How does that sound?"

Penny asked, "Can we switch papers if we don't like what we get?"

"If you can find someone willing to switch with you," Emma agreed.

"Can we put on music?" Pippa asked.

"I have a playlist on my phone, or if you have a radio we can find a station you all like."

Penny and Pippa seemed enthused. Paris didn't. In fact, as they went about their chores, then stopped to make lunch with food in the stocked refrigerator, and eventually finished vacuuming and dusting, Paris seemed unnaturally quiet compared to her more vibrant sisters. Emma wasn't exactly sure what to do about that. How would one get through to an eleven-year-old?

To Emma's surprise, Daniel's vehicle came rolling into the driveway around four o'clock. After he came in the door, Pippa ran to him and jumped into his arms. He hugged her and then set her down, but she was already chattering. "Emma says we can go see Fiesta since we finished the chores."

"She did, did she?" Daniel asked.

Emma stepped forward. Daniel's face was blank and she couldn't tell if he approved or not. "The girls helped me clean and dust, so I told them we could go see Fiesta. Do you want to come along?"

"Give me five minutes to change. We can take my SUV because we'll all fit."

True to his word, Daniel was back in five minutes in jeans and a red T-shirt. Emma felt that tingle inside of her when their gazes met. She couldn't help but notice his muscles under the T-shirt, his long legs, the way his hair fell over his brow.

Before she could notice anything else, she said, "Are we ready?"

They all piled into Daniel's SUV, with Emma sitting in the front and Daniel's daughters in the back. At first silence reigned but then Penny informed her dad, "Emma says we need to dust at least once a week. If we don't, we might sneeze and get a runny nose."

Daniel chuckled and glanced at Emma. "I know dusting is important, but it's the last thing on my to-do list every week."

"I can certainly understand that," Emma responded. "I'm sure you'd rather spend the time with your daughters."

"The thing is," Daniel said in a lower voice, "sometimes work interferes with that, too."

Soon Pippa was telling Daniel about the music they'd played while they were working and how they'd danced to it. Then she amended, "Penny and me did. Paris didn't dance. She didn't sing along, either."

Yes, Emma needed to talk to Daniel about Paris—about more than her quietness.

Once they'd parked in the shelter's parking lot, all three girls jumped out of the car and ran inside.

"I don't think they really want to be here, do you?" Daniel asked with a grin.

Emma unfastened her seat belt. Maybe the time to talk was now, when they were alone.

"That's the most excitement I've seen from Paris all day. She seems to really care about Fiesta. But there's more going on than her being quiet and reserved. I was a bit worried at lunchtime. I made sandwiches for them all but Paris only ate the lettuce and the ham and left the bread."

"She believes she has to watch her diet," Daniel said.

That didn't sound right to Emma. A girl Paris's age who kept active shouldn't need to watch what she ate, especially not if the food was good for her. However, Daniel didn't seem concerned, so maybe she should let the issue drop.

Daniel unfastened his seat belt and Emma couldn't help but notice he had large hands and brown hair on his way-too-masculine forearms. She switched her thoughts away from Daniel and back to Paris. "Paris was quiet all day. As Pippa said, she didn't join in while we were enjoying ourselves. I know maybe she's just quiet but I also wondered if she doesn't like another woman in the house."

Now Daniel turned to look at Emma. His jaw was set and his eyes held no warmth. "Nannies, housekeepers and babysitters have never bothered Paris, and basically, that's what I've hired you to be. Not a dietician or a psychologist. Just be their nanny, Emma, and we'll all get along just fine."

When Daniel opened his door to climb out, Emma told herself she shouldn't feel hurt. However, she did feel put in her place. She knew exactly what she had to do about that.

Emma waited until that evening, when Daniel's daughters were in bed on the second floor, to do what she had to do. Leaving her suite, she didn't hesitate to go to Daniel's office. The door was partially open and she rapped on it, making sure she had a good grip on her tablet in her other hand.

"Come in," Daniel called, with obvious surprise in his voice. "Are you a night owl, too?" he asked with a smile, apparently forgetting the annoyance he'd seemed to feel toward her that afternoon.

"No, not a night owl. I just wanted to talk to you without the girls around."

He stood, his eyebrows raised in question. "Are you feeling overwhelmed already?"

She came just inside the door and stood her ground. "No, I don't feel overwhelmed, but I do have a question."

"Ask away," he said in that deep baritone that practically made her toes curl.

She swallowed hard and held up her tablet. "I'd like to know exactly what my nanny duties are. I wouldn't want to overstep the boundaries again."

Daniel's expression changed. At first it was stoic and then understanding seemed to dawn on his face. "Emma—" he began.

However, she made herself clear again. "I don't want there to be any misunderstandings."

Daniel took a few steps closer to her. He was standing right in front of her. She noticed the curling chest hair at his neck in the *V* of his shirt, the way the shirt was tucked into his slim waist, the way his belt buckle hit a spot just below his navel.

"I'm sorry that your feelings were hurt with what I said about Paris. I don't want you worrying about her. That's not *your* job, it's *mine*."

"I'm probably going to be spending more time with her than you will," Emma reminded him.

He grimaced. "I know that, and every day I wake up planning to spend more time with them and something interferes. It's usually work-related, and I feel guilty."

"As long as you do the best you can and love them, you shouldn't feel guilty."

He ran his hand up and down the back of his neck. "I guess I wasn't raised that way. My father and mother taught me a sense of responsibility. They were strict but usually fair. That's ingrained in me."

"And you want to raise your daughters the same way."

"Not exactly the same way. I'd like to be less rigid."

"I don't think you're rigid," Emma said.

He laughed. "You've only spent a short time with me and the girls."

"Yes, but I noticed how caring you were about Fiesta. And today when I suggested you go along with us to the shelter, you readily agreed. There's nothing rigid in that."

Daniel was looking down at her so intently that her breath caught. In fact, she had the vague impression that he was leaning toward her and she was leaning toward him. If she raised her head and he bent his—

"No."

She hadn't realized she'd said it out loud until Daniel asked, "No?"

She cleared her throat and prattled, "No parent knows if he's doing exactly the right thing. But this is your family, and you are the one who decides how it's run. And I want to make sure I follow your rules. So can you tell me what my duties are?"

Then she was going to run back to her room and lock herself in. There were too many vibrations between her and this man, too much chemistry, and she was not going to do anything impulsive. She'd promised herself that, the day she'd found herself in Spring Forest, North Carolina, with no place to go and no one to help.

Daniel didn't step away but he did lift his hand with one finger raised. "Look after Paris, Penny and Pippa's physical needs. If a problem crops up or you think there's something to worry about, I *do* want you to tell me."

"You didn't appreciate me telling you about Paris," she reminded him.

"I know." He rubbed his fingers across his jaw—a very chiseled jaw, with a small cleft in the center. "I think I acted defensively because I've noticed the same things, but I don't know what to do about her. She's not eating as much as she should for a girl of her age. She wants to take part in summer swim-team activities so she doesn't gain weight."

"Are you going to let her be part of the team?"

"Yes, and that's something I'd like you to schedule. I negotiated with her. She's also to choose one of the camps at the community college. They have them for kids every summer. I'll give you their website address and maybe you can set that up, too. So the second point on my list of your duties would be arranging activities and chauffeuring them back and forth from the camps to home."

"When you say *camps*, do you mean like camping outside in tents?"

He chuckled. "No, not at all, though I suppose there is one that does that. These are educational camps. Someone qualified teaches them. The college accepts only so many children in each camp so the girls might not get their favorites. It's late to sign them up. Just do the best you can with it. I'll print out the info you need and give it to you in the morning."

She pointed to her tablet, where she'd typed in what he'd said. "That's only two duties."

"Chauffeuring is going to take up a good bit of your time. The third duty would be to keep the house in order, but that's a lower priority. If the girls would rather do some activity and you want to do it with them, I'd rather you do that than clean. They're off school for the summer and have a few chores to do. But mostly I want them to enjoy it. If actually cleaning the house becomes a problem, I'll hire someone to do that."

She was close enough to Daniel that she could easily see the lines around his eyes. Were those lines from looking into the sun or from laughing with his girls? From working too hard, poring over legal papers? Or from his divorce? That was too personal to comment on so she thought about the next thing she wanted to ask him. "I'd like to still volunteer at the shelter, if you think that's possible."

"I want you to make time for that if that's what you want to do. When I'm home, don't feel you have to spend time with my daughters. If there's something else you'd rather do, even if it's just reading in your room, then that's what you should do. I don't want to be rigid with you, either, Emma."

She felt her face getting warm because they were gazing into each other's eyes. Her heart seemed to be beating so loud she wondered if he could hear it. He had a look on his face that made her want to move closer to him, but she didn't. She wouldn't. She couldn't.

Starting tomorrow she'd ignore his attractiveness. She'd try to forget what she felt for him and his life here without his ex-wife and with his girls to raise on his own. Starting tomorrow, she'd truly be starting over. That's exactly what she wanted.

Chapter Four

Emma was surprised the following day when her cell phone buzzed and she saw the caller was Rebekah.

She answered. "Hi, Rebekah. Do you want me to come in? I could probably do an evening shift. I'm working as a nanny for Daniel Sutton now."

"So you got the job! Congratulations."

"I moved in yesterday. What can I help you with?"

"I'd like to talk to you about Fiesta. She needs more TLC than the shelter workers can give her. The vet examined her again when we saw her limping. He thinks her back leg was injured at some time. It has healed as much as it's going to—it still could bother her, though. And the worst part is, she's not eating as she should. She needs nourishment for herself and those kittens. Is there any way you could take her?"

"I just don't know. I'd have to talk to everyone here

about Fiesta. Daniel isn't too keen on bringing a pregnant cat in."

"I understand. See what you can do and then give me a call."

"Thank you, Rebekah. For everything."

When Emma put her cell phone back in her pocket, Pippa, Penny and even Paris were standing there looking up at her.

Should she tell them or shouldn't she?

Paris was the first to speak. "You mentioned Fiesta. Is something wrong?"

"You look upset," Penny added.

Pippa took hold of Emma's hand. That simple gesture brought tears to her eyes.

"The situation is that Fiesta needs extra care. The vet says she's not eating like she should. I'm not sure what to do. Do you think any of your friends would want to take in a pregnant cat?"

Penny jumped up and down. "*We* want to take her in. *We* want Fiesta."

"Your dad doesn't," Emma reminded them.

"But if we ask him real nice, he might. And if you back us up, that would clinch it," Paris added.

Emma wasn't sure that Paris's plan was the route to take, but the three girls cared about the cat and she did, too. There was no harm in asking. At least that's what she thought…until they asked.

That night no one said anything until after they'd finished dinner. Daniel had appreciated the meat loaf, macaroni and cheese and green beans. They both watched Paris as she nibbled, a little bit of this and a little bit of that.

When Emma served fresh strawberries over vanilla

ice cream, Daniel grinned at her. "I haven't had anything like this in a long time."

"Then enjoy it," she said as Pippa, Penny and Paris all gazed at her as if asking, "Can we ask him now?"

Emma gave a little nod.

As the oldest, Paris started. "Dad, we want to talk to you about something."

He took another bite of ice cream. "Sure. Anything."

Penny chimed in next. "Emma got a phone call today and it upset her. It upset us, too, when she told us about it."

Daniel's gaze shot to Emma's. "Did you have bad news from home?"

"No," Emma said softly. "It was Rebekah from the shelter. Fiesta is having a few problems."

Pippa explained exactly what those problems were. As she did, Daniel frowned, and then he scowled. That scowl was meant for Emma.

"Won't you let us bring her home, Dad?" Paris begged.

Pippa went to her dad and gave him a hug. "Please, Daddy. We'll get to see her kittens born."

Penny sounded like an old soul when she said, "It would mean a lot to us, Dad."

Daniel studied each of his daughters, one by one. He didn't look at Emma. "We do have a spare room upstairs. We could keep her in there, at least until after the kittens are born."

All three of his daughters cheered, high-fived and gave Emma wide smiles. Then Daniel said, "Why don't you go up to your rooms for a while. I'd like to talk to Emma."

His daughters were now ready to do anything he said.

They ran off talking about preparations for Fiesta and exactly what they'd put in her room.

As soon as Daniel heard all three girls run up the stairs, he pointed his finger at Emma. "You ambushed me."

"I didn't," Emma protested, feeling defensive. "It happened exactly as your daughters said. What were they supposed to do, write you a letter so you didn't feel ambushed?"

"You could have called me at work to warn me that this was coming. Instead, all three came at me at once with you managing in the background."

"I wasn't managing anything. The girls have felt strongly about Fiesta ever since they found her."

He shook his head, scowling again. "You shouldn't have talked to them about the cat until you consulted with me. They've had enough loss. What if Fiesta or one of the kittens dies? On the other hand, if the kittens are healthy, I have to find homes for them and the mom. I don't want a houseful of cats."

Emma had kept her temper even up until now. But suddenly his words lit a match to it. She pushed her chair away from the table and stood. "If I'm going to be involved in your daughters' all-day care, then that means I'm going to be involved in their lives. I wasn't going to tell them what the phone call was about but they heard Fiesta's name mentioned. I wasn't going to lie to them when they asked me about it. And as we talked about it, I realized a pregnant cat could teach them about birth and responsibility. It could also bond you with your daughters more than they are now. Did you ever think of that?"

Before she cried in front of him, she tossed her napkin to the table. "I'll clear this mess later. I'm going to my room for a little while."

She hurried from the kitchen before more of her feelings leaked out.

Daniel cleaned off the table and ran the dishwasher. Action was his defense against unsettled feelings. Emma Alvarez had unsettled quite a few. When he'd finished all the kitchen chores—he was not going to leave them for Emma—he knew what he had to do.

Apologizing wasn't something that came easy to him. Maybe that was one of the reasons Lydia had left, along with many others. Unfortunately, Emma's actions had stirred up the past. It was a hornet's nest he didn't usually disturb. Possibly, that's why he still felt empty sometimes. After Lydia had left, he'd had to focus on the girls and work. That was it. It was called putting one foot in front of the other and he'd done that for two years.

However, suddenly Emma's presence had thrust him back into thoughts of his marriage and the aftermath of it. He was uncomfortable. That's why he'd argued with Emma.

Walking down the hall to her room, he knew there was a possibility that she could be packing to leave. Did she run from arguments? Did she stay and fight? Did she resolve them and go on? He didn't know how she would respond to their current problem. To his surprise, he wanted to find the answers to all of those questions.

Knocking on Emma's door, he tried to prepare himself for the scene ahead. After all, that's what lawyers did. *Don't ask a question you don't know the answer to.* At least that's what his friends who were criminal-trial lawyers had told him.

When Emma opened the door, her eyes went wide. She obviously hadn't expected him. She'd changed into a sleeping tank and shorts that had little multicolored paws all over them. That almost made him smile. But the discussion they had to have was too serious.

"I'd like to talk to you," he said.

She shored herself up to her full height and squared her shoulders. Maybe she thought he was going to fire her. No chance of that. "Can I come in?" he asked.

She looked as if she wanted to say no, but she didn't. Rather, she stepped back so he could walk into the room. He told himself he should keep his distance. Instead of taking his own advice, he motioned to the love seat. "Can we sit?"

"I suppose," she answered warily.

After they were both seated and she managed to position herself at least five inches away from him, he plunged right in. "I'm sorry for what I said earlier."

Her voice was soft when she responded, "I shouldn't have answered you the way I did. You're my employer and—"

He interrupted, "Employer or not, I want you to be honest with me. I want to tell you why I became so defensive."

Her expression gentled and so did the look in her liquid brown eyes. "Daniel, you don't have to do that."

"I think I do. Maybe you'll understand me and my daughters better if I explain."

"All right." She still sounded hesitant about it, and he wondered if she didn't want to know much about him so he wouldn't ask questions about *her*. That was a subject for another time.

"My ex-wife often made decisions on her own that

affected all of us. The last one she made was leaving her family."

Emma studied his face. "You didn't see it coming?"

The corners of his lips turned down and the lines on his brow deepened. "No. I'm not sure what that says about me as a husband, but I didn't see it coming. My law partner's name was Allen. The two of us had won a class action suit against a medical-device manufacturer that captured national recognition for us. We were both offered jobs in a prestigious law firm in Alexandria, Virginia. Lydia and I discussed it. She wanted me to take the job, but I wanted our daughters to grow up in a small town where everyone knew and cared about everybody else."

"I've seen that since I came here," Emma agreed. "Everyone in the town appears concerned for everyone else."

He nodded, then went on. "I rejected the offer from the law firm but Allen accepted it. That offer doubled his salary. Lydia ran away with him because she wanted a different life than I did. That trumped leaving her daughters behind. I also learned she'd been having an affair with him."

Emma reached out and covered his hand with hers. "I'm so sorry. Does Lydia stay in touch with the girls?"

"She sends them cards on their birthdays. She called this past Christmas. But afterward, Pippa had nightmares again. Penny complained that they never see their mom so they really don't have one. Paris was even more quiet than usual for the week after the call. Pippa has asked me more than once if her mommy still loves her. I don't know what to say to that."

"Daniel…"

"I didn't tell you this so you'd feel sorry for me or the

girls. We're doing good. But I want you to understand where we're coming from. You're right about being in the girls' lives day-to-day more than I am. I'll try to be open-minded. I still don't know about bringing a pregnant cat into the house but we'll deal with it." He gave her a wry smile and felt himself leaning toward her.

Emma smiled back and assured him, "I'll consult with you about big decisions."

They were very close as he said, "How about if you define *big*."

Before they realized it, their lips were an inch apart and then finally just a breath apart. This time Daniel couldn't have pulled away if he'd wanted to. A fantastically sensual power seemed to overtake them both. His mouth took hers with a vehemence that astonished him and maybe astonished her. However, instead of pulling away, she returned the same pressure. Just his lips on hers made him want so much more.

Suddenly common sense dumped cold water on him. He leaned away and so did she. "Well," he said, "I'm not going to apologize for that, but I know that getting involved would be a big mistake."

"Are you saying the kiss was a mistake?" Emma asked him, her eyes bright.

"What do you think?"

"We shouldn't let it happen again," she agreed. "Not if I want to work here. I don't intend to get involved with anyone for a long, long time."

As she said that, her voice shook a little. Daniel suspected her last romance had hurt her deeply. "I'm not ready for an involvement, either, but that doesn't mean we can't be friends, right?"

As soon as he said the word, he knew he was kidding

himself. He could see her breasts rising and falling under the cute tank top. Her lips had that just-kissed look. If he wasn't the father of three girls who needed him to make responsible decisions, he'd take Emma into his arms and kiss her again.

That wasn't what friendship was about. He held out his hand to her and she put hers in it. He squeezed her hand and reiterated, "Friends."

But after they said good-night and he'd left Emma's room, he was sure *friends* wasn't the right word for what seemed to be beginning between them.

The next morning, as usual, Daniel was up early. The sun had come up and the birds had started tweeting as he dressed for the office. But when he exited his bedroom he heard scrambling and low talking in the room down the hall. Passing by Paris's room, and then Pippa's and Penny's, who shared one, he saw that their doors were open. Their beds were unmade, but this early that wasn't unusual. Making their beds was one of the chores they had to do every day. As a responsible parent, he still wasn't sure which chores were necessary and which weren't. But even Pippa could take care of that one.

He walked down the hall and stopped in front of the closed door. Hearing voices inside, he opened it slowly, not knowing what to expect. He would have thought his daughters and Emma would still be sleeping this early.

What he saw inside made him stop and recalculate. The single bed in the room, ready for Penny when she decided she wanted a separate room from her sister, had been pushed up against one wall. He recognized the blanket that had been tossed on top of it. It was from the linen closet.

Emma, in jeans and a T-shirt, her feet bare, was kneeling on the floor adjusting a large plastic bin. He could see through the side. There was torn paper on the bottom and a towel laid across that. Paris was positioning an old rug she must have found in the basement under the bin. Penny and Pippa were nestling a towel in a carton and they pushed it inside the open closet.

Not exactly sure how to deal with what they were doing, he simply stated, "I'm sure there's a reason you're up this early."

Penny answered him. "As soon as Furever Paws opens, we want to go get Fiesta. First, we have to go to the pet store and buy a cat carrier, food, a litter box and litter. That's what the website said."

He raised his eyebrows at Emma. "What website?"

"Furever Paws has a page on their website that lists the supplies you need if you're going to bring a cat home. I let the girls use my tablet and we found the items we might need for a pregnant cat."

From her position in the closet, Pippa explained, "Sometimes the momma cat likes to have her babies in the dark, in a quiet place. So we're putting a box in the closet, too."

"Too?" he asked.

This time Paris answered, "She'll have a choice."

"Even if she has a choice, she'll probably go under the bed to have them," he proclaimed wryly. After all, cats could be as unpredictable as kids.

"No, she won't, Dad," Pippa protested. "We'll keep showing her the best place to go. She'll listen."

Emma rose to her feet. "The girls said you wouldn't mind if we rearranged the room."

"*I* said that," Penny confirmed. "It's supposed to be

my room someday, so I can do with it what I want. Right, Dad?"

Sometimes he was absolutely amazed at children's logic. And yet, he found no good reason to object to the changes, at least not for now. "I suppose you'll need a feeding area, too. Don't forget bowls when you go to the pet store."

Paris, the practical one, said, "Dad, we're going to need some money."

"I can chip in," Emma said quietly.

"And I can empty my piggy bank," Pippa agreed.

He took out his wallet. "No one has to empty their piggy bank. Emma, I don't expect you to chip in." He took bills from his wallet and handed them to Emma. "I'll leave it up to you to calculate the budget. For now, I have to go."

"Do you always go to the office this early?" Emma asked.

"That depends on if I have a sitter for the girls."

Emma turned to his daughters. "You finish arranging. I want to talk to your dad for a few minutes. I'll be back."

The girls were already talking about the best places for the feeding station and toys they might want to buy.

Emma preceded Daniel out the door and they walked down the hall. Daniel was aware of a flower fragrance that always seemed to surround her. He wondered if it was perfume or maybe shampoo. Whatever it was, he liked it. He not only liked it, but his body also responded to it.

Standing close at the top of the stairs, he longed to run his hand through her hair. It was so curly and glossy, and he could imagine it spread across his pillow.

No. He would *not* imagine that. "What did you want to talk to me about?"

"Fixing up the room was the girls' idea. I heard them clomping up and down the stairs. They were going in and out of the garage."

"The storage area," Daniel murmured.

"Yes. There were boxes, old blankets and bins scattered about. They were taking what they needed for the room. I decided if I supervised, maybe they wouldn't wake you."

"Never worry about waking me." Then he added, "Not when it has to do with the girls."

"I was concerned this was one of those decisions we should have talked about together."

"Oh, you think this is a *big* one?" He chuckled. "You don't know Penny, Pippa and Paris yet if you think this was a big undertaking. They'll surprise you with their creativity."

This time Emma laughed. Then she sobered. "So you're okay with us going to the pet store and picking up Fiesta at the shelter without you?"

Suddenly, he *did* want to go along with them, but that was unnecessary.

"The girls need a little adventure in their lives. With me, that could be swimming, hiking, miniature golf. But with *you*, something like this seems perfect."

Right now, gazing into Emma's brown eyes, *she* seemed perfect. He couldn't help himself when he said, "You look pretty this morning."

"Really?" she joked. "I'd barely washed my face and brushed my teeth when I heard the girls."

In spite of himself, in spite of all his good intentions, he reached out and wrapped one of her curls around his index finger. It was so soft. "You don't need makeup, fancy clothes or jewelry to look pretty."

They stared at each other while the vibrations zipped between them. He knew he was courting trouble, but something about Emma got to him. Fighting it once more, he drew back his hand.

"If you need me, don't hesitate to call me. I have one client appointment this morning at ten. Other than that, I'll be working at my desk."

"All right," she said in such a soft voice he could hardly hear her.

Then he jogged down the stairs before he found out for sure if she was as attracted to him as he was to her.

Chapter Five

Emma heard the sound of the girls scurrying in and out of the bedroom upstairs. The day had grown considerably warmer. Thank goodness Daniel's house had air-conditioning. This morning, to the girls' chagrin, Emma, Paris, Penny and Pippa had gone to the grocery store and the pet store for supplies. Then they'd taken those items home before they finally drove to Furever Paws. After they'd brought Fiesta home, they'd spent almost the whole day there. Because of Fiesta and their attention to her, Emma had decided to make something easy for supper—tacos. Daniel's daughters had said they liked them.

Emma had just turned the ground meat and sauce down to a simmer when she heard the front door open. Crossing to the foyer, she saw it was Daniel. But not just Daniel. He'd carried in a huge cat condo and set it down. It had four shelves and a cube at the bottom that kittens could hide in.

"What's this?" she asked with a teasing smile.

"You know full well what it is. I thought it might come in handy for Fiesta and her kittens. I suppose we'll have to keep them for a while before we can give them away."

"Twelve weeks is good," Emma informed him.

Daniel gave a low whistle. "That long?"

She laughed. "You'll soon be used to kittens climbing up your jeans."

He looked speechless and she laughed again. Keeping the condo where it stood, he approached her slowly and came very close. He was a good six inches taller than she was. She tipped up her chin. Her heart was beating so fast she found it hard to swallow.

Concentrating on something concrete, she said in a whispery voice, "The vet says Fiesta could deliver in ten days or less. The three P's have spent most of the day in the room with her."

"Doing what?"

"You really aren't a cat or dog person, are you?" Emma asked with a frown, hoping that would break the magnetic pull between them.

Apparently, Daniel didn't take her frown seriously. "I'll certainly find out soon if I'm a cat person."

She couldn't hold the frown. "They've been petting her, watching her nap, playing games on their electronic devices while they keep her company. Pippa took her coloring book and crayons into the room with her. I think Penny was devising new soccer plays."

"You know, we could put a cat cam or even one of those baby monitors in the room. Then you'll know or hear what's going on," Daniel suggested.

"I don't want to feel like I'm spying on the girls."

Daniel shook his head and smiled, and then took Emma's chin in his hand. "You *would* think of that. I was just imagining watching and hearing Fiesta—then we'd know when she delivers."

Emma felt her face heat. "I guess you're wondering why I jumped to that conclusion."

"That I'd want to spy on my daughters?"

Emma nodded. She hesitated because she didn't share personal information easily. Especially since her disastrous relationship. But she was feeling close to Daniel and so she explained, "After my mom died, my father watched me like a hawk. I think he was afraid something would happen to me, too, especially as I grew older. I hated the feeling that he was hovering all the time. I never really had fun when I went to a party or even a gathering of friends because I was worried he was worrying."

"You couldn't just be a kid, a normal teenager."

"I'm not sure how normal teenagers are," Emma commented.

Gazing into her eyes, Daniel said, "You're one of the most down-to-earth women I've ever met."

She wrinkled her nose. "I'm not sure that's a compliment."

"Oh, it is," he assured her. For a moment—just a moment—she thought he was going to kiss her. Did she want him to?

The thought was interrupted by a rap on the front door.

Startled, they both stepped apart. When Daniel saw who was at the door, he groaned. "It's my sister, Shannon. She said she wanted to meet you. I told her we'd invite her for dinner some night, but I haven't done it yet."

Emma heard the chagrin in his tone and rushed to re-assure him. "There will be plenty of taco shells and fill-ing. She's welcome to join us."

"She has her three-year-old with her."

"I like children," Emma reminded him.

Emma peered through the glass of the storm door and saw Shannon holding her little boy's hand. "He's adorable."

"Ian is three. Ever since Shannon lost Cameron a year ago, she's devoted all of her time and attention to Ian."

"She's jiggling the doorknob."

Daniel grimaced. "I better let her in before she breaks the door down. That's the kind of woman Shannon is."

Emma was suddenly glad she had a thumbnail sketch of Daniel's sister. Hopefully that would help her avoid any faux pas.

Preparing dinner, Emma tried to keep her mind on what she was doing. That was tough when she felt both Daniel's and Shannon's eyes on her. They hadn't called Penny, Pippa and Paris into the kitchen yet. Emma had started referring to them as the three P's, and Daniel seemed to like it.

He also seemed to like the sizzle between them. That was the only word she could think of.

As she brought down the knife blade on the lettuce, she almost cut her finger. She had to keep her attention focused on chopping up tomatoes and lettuce for the tacos and *not* on her handsome boss.

"Are you sure there isn't anything I can do?" Shan-non asked.

Emma glanced at Shannon, who had beautiful auburn

curls and a ready smile for her son. Ian was opening up Daniel's bottom kitchen cupboards.

Should she give his sister something to do? "Would you like to grate the cheese?"

"I usually buy the packs where they're already grated," Daniel's sister told her.

"I do sometimes," Emma agreed.

"And not others?" Shannon questioned.

Pushed by Shannon, Emma responded, "I think the cheese tastes fresher and has more flavor when I buy the block and then grate it."

"I see," Shannon said thoughtfully, and Emma saw her exchange a look with her brother.

Trying to turn the conversation back to Shannon, Emma commented, "Daniel told me you work at home. You design adult coloring books, the ones with the mandalas and flowers and patterns, right?"

"That's right. I've been fortunate," Shannon said. "I found a company who likes my work."

"I've always wanted to try coloring," Emma said.

"You *will* have to try it sometime," Shannon replied.

Emma went to the refrigerator, found the block of cheese, unwrapped it and set it on a cutting board with the grater. "I think we make time for what's most important to us. I always volunteered at animal shelters and that takes up my spare time."

"I see. Daniel said you brought a cat home."

Daniel had been sitting by, watching the interplay. Now he cut in. "*We* did. It was what the girls wanted, so we all agreed. Fiesta's in the upstairs bedroom. Maybe we can take Ian up to see her after supper."

"A cat?" Shannon wrinkled her nose. "I've always

considered dogs, but he's not old enough to have much responsibility for an animal."

"That's why I agreed to let the three P's bring home Fiesta."

"The three P's?" Shannon asked. "Since when did that start?"

"Since Emma arrived. She adds imagination to their days. She even got them to help her clean the house."

"Wow, you must be a miracle worker."

Emma shrugged. "A little music goes a long way in livening up chores that usually aren't a whole lot of fun. We made a game of it. They'd each pick a task and who-ever got done first got to pick the next type of music."

"And they danced," Daniel added. "I would have liked to have seen that."

This time Emma's gaze collided with his, and she knew he meant those words. The idea of him watching her dance, if you wanted to call it that, was highly sensual.

Shannon looked from one of them to the other as Emma turned back to slicing tomatoes. Emma caught sight of Shannon elbowing her brother. Shannon didn't seem very happy with Emma's presence here. She hoped she wasn't going to cause a rift between them.

Shannon's little boy came running over to her with a small saucepan in his hands that he'd pulled from the cupboard. He tapped on Emma's leg.

She wiped off her hands and crouched down to his eye level. "How can I help you, little man?"

"Spoon," he said, pointing to the ceramic jar that held kitchen utensils.

Daniel explained, "He uses a spoon and the pot to create music."

Emma selected a wooden serving spoon, then

crouched down again and handed it to him. "How about this one? It will make a thumping noise instead of a clanging sound."

Ian took it, smiled mischievously at her, then banged the spoon on the pot. It didn't make the sound he expected and he looked totally surprised.

"I told you she was smart," Daniel said to his sister.

Shannon's little boy thumped the spoon on the pot again and then giggled.

"Not only is she a miracle worker with your girls, but she seems to have the magic touch with toddlers, too," Shannon commented. "What did you say you did before you came to North Carolina?"

Emma returned the little boy's smile and then straightened. "I was an office manager, but I also supervised local playground activities for a couple of summers. Running a household doesn't seem that much different to me."

"If you were a mom, it might," Shannon suggested.

"Shannon—" Daniel warned. Then, to cut the tension in the room, he pushed back his chair and stood. "I'll call the girls. I'm sure they'd like to help fill the tacos."

"By all means," Shannon said. "We'll see how Emma handles the three-ring circus in the kitchen."

Emma could have responded but she didn't. She knew when to hold her tongue. She also knew when to concentrate on kids rather than adults. Shannon was obviously testing her. Daniel kept looking her way and Emma felt confusion at that.

Yes, it was better to concentrate on the children. She wouldn't get into trouble doing that.

Emma tossed and turned that night. She knew if she fell asleep she'd dream about Daniel. She'd never had X-rated dreams before, and she shouldn't be having them now. Should she quit as his nanny? But she needed the income, and it was a good position, even including housing so she could mostly save her salary.

The following morning after Daniel left, Emma made breakfast for the girls—bacon and pancakes. Then she sat down with them to go over the camps that the community college was offering and to register them. The sessions would start on Monday. Daniel thought the camps were important for out-of-the-box educational experiences. As Emma looked down over the list, she saw exactly why. She read off the camps in different age groups.

Pippa made a choice without hardly thinking about it—"Jewels to wear and share." She was jumping up and down with excitement just thinking about it. "I can make a bracelet for each of us, or maybe necklaces, too."

"Maybe you'll just be making one thing for you. You'll have to wait and see," Emma suggested.

"I'm sure whatever it is, it will be pretty and special."

Next, Emma read off the list for Penny's age group. Emma was surprised when Penny didn't choose sports camp but selected "Making Duct-Tape Art."

"That will really stretch your imagination," Emma said, holding back her smile.

"It will be cool," Penny said. "Did you see all the colors and patterns they make duct tape in now? I can't wait."

"I guess I have to look at the list, too," Paris said with no enthusiasm. "I just want to belong to the swim team and go swimming at the community pool."

"Let's make a deal," Emma advised. "In addition to your team practice sessions and your camp, we'll all go swimming one day a week, weather permitting, if you choose a camp, too."

Paris gave a very loud but ultimately resigned sigh. However, when she looked down the list on Emma's tablet, she pointed to one right away. "I've always wanted to make a video game. Do you think I could really learn that?"

"The description on the website says every camp student will complete a project."

Paris motioned to Emma's tablet screen. "Are we finished with the registering now?"

"What would you like to do?"

"I'd just like to go upstairs and spend some time with Fiesta. She's got to be lonely up there alone."

"Maybe she is. I'm sure she'll be glad for your company, and you can keep an eye on her and watch for signs that she might have her kittens soon. Remember what the signs are?"

"Meowing more," Penny said.

"Nesting," Paris added. "Pawing into the paper or the towel we have in her bins."

"Looking around for someplace to have her babies," Pippa said.

"That's all correct—good job remembering. We should probably put a sheet under the bed just in case she does start looking for another nesting place. Come on, I'll find one for you."

The day passed quickly until Daniel came home. As always, Penny and Pippa ran to hug him. Paris just said, "Hi, Dad."

On some level, Emma wondered if Paris blamed Daniel for her mom leaving. Did they know the full story? Did they know why Lydia had left?

After supper that evening, the three P's were watching TV. Emma took the sign-up sheets she'd printed from her tablet. Daniel had given her permission to use his printer. She found him in his office. His door was wide open, but she still rapped lightly.

He swiveled around in his chair. "Hi, Emma. What's up?"

"I have the confirmation sheets for the girls' camps."

He took the papers from her hand. "Let me see what they chose."

As he looked over the classes, he grinned. "Pippa's is the only one that makes real sense. She likes shiny crystals. Duct-tape art for Penny? That's surprising. And how much argument did Paris give you about going at all?"

"We made a deal."

"My guess is you got the short end of the stick."

Emma laughed. "Not necessarily. In addition to her swim practices, I told her we'd go to the pool one day a week. She seems to be into the idea of making a video game. The camps last until 2:00 p.m. Does all of this work with your schedule?"

"Yes, it does." After he set the printouts on his desk, he said, "I have something I want to ask *you*, too."

Her gaze collided with his and her heart started bumping a phenomenally loud rhythm—so loud that she wondered if he could hear. He'd changed into a black-and-white football jersey and black jean shorts. His feet were bare and so were hers. But her tank top and shorts felt kind of skimpy as he studied her. Sometimes she felt as if he could see right through her. That scared her as much as it excited her.

She found her voice and asked, "What did you want to know?"

"Do you think you'll have any spare time?"

She didn't exactly know how her schedule was going to work out yet. "Why do you want to know?"

"My secretary is leaving for two weeks to visit her sister in Arkansas. They're going to look at retirement homes for their parents. During those two weeks I really need an office manager, not only for an organized office, but to start a search for an associate in the firm. I'd bump up your salary if you can do that while the girls are at camp."

Working in Daniel's law office would give her more job experience for her résumé, and she'd be able to put more money in the bank. Not only that, but it would also sound more stable than being a nanny when she told her father about it. The last time she spoke with him she hadn't told him about the boyfriend fiasco, but she had informed him she was searching for a job. Of course, he'd wanted her to come home. She was determined not to do that.

"So I'd be working the front desk?"

"Yes, you would. I can teach you how to work the intercom system. Why do you ask?"

Feeling awkward, she didn't know what to say. She felt her cheeks getting red.

She had ducked her chin and now Daniel inched toward her and looked up into her face. "Come on, Emma, tell me what's wrong."

"Nothing's wrong, exactly."

"But you'd rather work in the reception area than next to me in my office?"

Now she'd done it. She'd insulted him. However, when she lifted her chin and looked at his face, he didn't look insulted.

"What are you afraid of, Emma?"

"We've kissed, and…" She stumbled over her words, feeling foolish. "I just want to make sure that while I'm working with you we have a professional relationship."

"We'll have a strictly professional relationship, Emma, if that's what you want."

The truth was…she wasn't sure *what* she wanted. She did know, however, she wasn't going to do anything impulsive. Their professional relationship would keep them both safe from a broken heart.

"I'm sorry if I insulted you," she apologized.

"No, you haven't. I'm glad you've made your feelings clear. That way, we won't have any misunderstandings. I admire you for doing that, Emma. So you will become my office manager for two weeks, at least in the mornings?"

"That sounds good." In order to leave his office, she came up with an excuse. "I'm going to call my dad now. I never gave him my new address. He'll be glad to know I'm settled and working."

When she turned to go, he caught her arm. She liked the feel of his fingers on her skin. She liked the way he smelled of leather and pine. She liked the twinkle in his eyes when he interacted with the three P's. And she loved the way she'd felt when he'd kissed her.

She looked up at him, not knowing what to expect.

"Emma, this situation is new to both of us. I've never had a housekeeper or a nanny like you."

"Like me?"

This time his cheeks took on a ruddiness that wasn't there before. "Yeah, like you. Pretty and smart and attractive to me in a way a woman hasn't been in a long time. I don't want you to ever feel uncomfortable. If something isn't to your liking, I want you to tell me."

"I will," she murmured as he released her arm. As she walked down the hall to her suite, she knew what *was* to her liking. Him.

About an hour later, Daniel thought about the job offer he'd given to Emma. The one thing he didn't want was for her to feel pressured to say yes. Maybe he should have explained that better.

Walking down the hall to her suite, he saw that her door was closed. He didn't think she would have gone to bed this early. Even the girls were still up.

He knocked.

She came to the door almost immediately. She was still dressed in her tank and shorts and obviously hadn't turned in yet. But when she opened the door and he saw her face, he knew she was troubled about something. It was either his job offer or her conversation with her father.

"What's wrong?" Maybe she'd be honest with him and he wouldn't have to guess.

"It's not your concern," she said with a shake of her head.

He should have been concentrating on her words, but instead he was concentrating on her very soft-looking lips. "I don't want you to feel I twisted your arm into taking my office job. If you feel I'm asking too much, it's fine to say no—it won't impact your job here as nanny."

She looked confused for a moment and then she said, "Oh, no. I don't feel that at all. It's an opportunity I really want to explore, even if it is only for two weeks."

"Then what's troubling you?" He kept from touching

her, though it was extremely difficult to keep his hands by his sides.

She crossed over to the love seat and sat on it. "I'm sure you don't want to get involved in my personal life."

If he didn't, he'd leave. If he did, he'd go over and sit beside her. That's what he did. "Who said I don't?"

Her eyes widened as their knees touched, skin to skin.

"Did your father have a problem with you staying here?"

"I didn't exactly tell him that I was. I told him I found a job in a lawyer's office as an office manager, but I'm also taking side jobs. I also explained about volunteering at the animal shelter."

"But not that you're a nanny?"

"No, not yet. I thought it was better to let him get used to one thing at a time."

"Which thing is he getting used to first?"

"That I want to stay in North Carolina and build a life here. I need to separate myself from my father's protectiveness."

Something about that sounded off to him, as if there was more she wasn't saying. After all, Daniel was a lawyer and he had lawyerly instincts. "Did something happen because of his protectiveness?"

"What happened was probably my attitude. Dad has always been cautious, wants to take everything step by step—*A* before *B*, *B* before *C*."

"What does your dad do?"

"He's a professor of Hispanic Studies at Penn State."

"Professors *are* logical," Daniel suggested.

"Yes, but it can go too far—especially when it comes to parenting. I began rebelling against his logic. I know, I'm a little too old to rebel. I wasn't even conscious I was doing it. I think I became more impulsive over the years because of his strict rules and rigid traditions."

Reaching out, Daniel laid his hand on Emma's arm. "Why did you come to North Carolina? Did you throw a dart at a map of the United States?"

She gave him a weak smile. "No, that's probably what I should have done instead of chasing after a man who didn't love me."

Whoa. Daniel hadn't expected that. Who wouldn't love Emma? He didn't stop to think why he'd come up with that question. He let his hand slide down to hers. "I'm a good listener."

When she eyed him warily, he thought maybe she'd picked up some of her dad's caution. Then she gave a little shrug. "Let me give credit where credit is due. My father never approved of John, though he couldn't give me a good reason why. In the past I'd respected my dad's opinion. Although he's a successful tenured professor and while he hears new ideas from his students every day, he's still old-school. His great-grandfather came to America from Mexico and worked on the railroad. His grandfather was an engineer and his father was an electrical engineer. My dad broke from tradition and worked his way through degrees until he earned his PhD in Hispanic Studies."

"He sounds like an accomplished man. And truthfully you can't blame him for being protective since you lost your mom."

"I know. But dating has always been an issue between us. And when he didn't particularly like John... Anyway, John and I had been dating about six months. He'd come to Pennsylvania to manage a start-up company. I met him at a conference and admired his ambition. I fell for his charm." She said this with an embarrassed glow coloring her cheeks.

"If he was working in Pennsylvania, how did you end up in North Carolina?"

"North Carolina was his home base, and he lived in Spring Forest. He insisted a long-distance romance would keep our relationship fresh and interesting. And at first, it seemed like it did. He would fly back to Pennsylvania or drive back fairly often. He never seemed to want me to fly down here. There was one spell of three weeks when he was too busy to visit for the weekend. I thought our relationship was becoming too difficult to sustain long-distance, so I decided to give up all for love. I quit my job, packed necessities in a suitcase, grabbed my messenger bag and drove down here to surprise him. But when I reached John's apartment, I realized I should have listened to my dad. John's *fiancée* answered the door. His fiancée! He'd never been serious about me. I'd simply been a distraction while he'd worked out of state."

Her eyes were glistening now and Daniel couldn't help but put his arms around her and draw her close. She leaned her head on his shoulder and took a few bolstering breaths. He wanted to kiss her but he didn't want to take advantage of her.

Instead, he just tightened his arms slightly and said, "I know what betrayal feels like, Emma. Believe me, I do."

When she turned to face him, their noses were almost touching. It would be so easy to lean in, taste her lips again...taste more.

But that wasn't what she needed right now and he probably didn't, either.

Seeming to recognize the need for some distance between them, she pulled out of the hug and out of his embrace. He was so sorry she did. She'd felt so good in his arms.

She was looking a bit more embarrassed. "I'm sorry I spilled all that out on you."

"No need to be sorry, Emma. I do understand. Although it's been two years since Lydia left, I still have regrets. I wonder what I could have done differently. I wonder now how I can make her communicate better with Pippa, Penny and Paris. About a year ago, I realized I have to let that go. I can foster a relationship between Lydia and the girls if that's what they all want, but I can't make it happen."

"It's tough when we have to admit we can't control everything, isn't it?"

"It certainly is. You know, don't you, that your dad just wants to control your life so that you're happy."

"I know, and I will tell him I'm a nanny. I just want to let the rest settle in first."

Daniel couldn't advise Emma on what was best for her. She had to figure that out on her own. He stood and so did she.

"Thank you," she said.

"I didn't do anything."

"You were right. You're a good listener. I'll have to remind your daughters of that from time to time."

Daniel laughed. "You do that." He headed for the door and closed it behind him.

His attraction to Emma Alvarez was growing in leaps and bounds. There had to be some way to put a stop to it.

Chapter Six

The following Monday, Emma began working in Daniel's office while the girls started their camps. She could work with Daniel from eight to two before picking them up. She thought about the weekend and the time they'd spent together. On Saturday she'd volunteered at Furever Paws. At supper on the patio that night, they'd shared a healthy meal of hamburgers, fresh tomatoes and zucchini cooked in a basket on the grill. The girls had played croquet in the yard. Paris had still been quiet but Emma couldn't say she was sullen. Emma had watched her eat, though, and had been disappointed to see that Paris had only eaten the grilled veggies and a slice of tomato, along with drinking a lot of water.

Emma caught on quickly to Raina's system in Daniel's office with the files of clients and the computer scheduling program. At 10:00 a.m. she'd made the list that Daniel needed of possible associates to hire. There was one name, one woman, who seemed particularly qualified. Emma circled Megan Jennings's name. Originally from New York City, now living in North Carolina, she had an undergraduate degree in finance in addition to her law degree.

Still unsure of what Daniel preferred—a knock on the door or a buzz of the intercom—she buzzed him. When he answered, he said, "Emma, you can come right in if there's something you need."

"I have something *you* need. I'll be right in."

When she entered Daniel's office, she saw that he was working on something on his computer. A brief, maybe? He swiveled his chair around and watched as she crossed the office to him. There was a sparkle in those green eyes that said he appreciated what he saw. She hadn't worn anything special. She really did have to go shopping for clothes. She'd dressed in a pair of white slacks with a yellow sleeveless cotton blouse.

Before she could present him with the list, he said, "Just looking at you makes me think of a summer day."

"Thank you," she returned, realizing in her heart that his compliment had been sincere.

She handed Daniel the list. Without hesitating, she advised, "I think your first interview should be Megan Jennings. She's qualified and she even lives in Spring Forest."

Daniel asked Emma about Megan's degrees and such, and then he nodded. "I'll trust your judgment on this since you've done the legwork. Can you set up an appointment with her? The sooner the better."

"Sure, no problem, if I can get hold of her. If I reach her voice mail, do you want me to leave your cell number?"

"You do think ahead," he noted with a grin. "I like

that. Yes, give her my cell number if you leave a message."

After Emma returned to her desk and left a message for Megan Jennings, she glanced out the window. She'd checked the Weather Channel and the temperature was going to go up. It would be a great day for swimming.

She leaned into Daniel's office again. "After I pick up the girls from their camps, I'd like to take them swimming. Would that be okay?"

"Sure, that's fine. It's a perfect day for swimming. Are you going to swim, too?" The expression on his face said he might be imagining her in a swimsuit.

"I might. I did pack my bathing suit when I came to Spring Forest though I need to shop for some other summer clothes. One of these days after camp I'd like to take the three P's shopping. They're definitely outgrowing their jeans."

Daniel looked disconcerted for a moment, picked up a pen on his desk and clicked it on and off a few times. Emma could tell he wanted to talk to her about something but seemed to be having trouble doing it. She waited.

Finally, he set down the pen. "I don't know whether to bring this up with you or not, but since you are going to take them shopping…"

"Yes? Is there something you want me to buy for them?"

"It's Paris. There's a subject I know she won't talk about with me, but you might be able to find out."

"Find out what?"

He blushed a little. "Find out if she thinks she needs a bra. It's just one of those conversations that I don't think dads and daughters are good at."

"No, they're not," Emma agreed. "I remember asking

my dad for money for clothes and he questioned me on what clothes I needed in particular. That's just the way he is. So I told him that I needed new bras. I wish you could have seen the expression on his face. He turned a color of red I've never seen before, and he was totally speechless. My dad, speechless. Never happened."

Daniel chuckled. "Is it awful of me not to want to go through that with Paris?"

"It would be wonderful if the two of you became comfortable enough to talk about something like that. But I do feel Paris isn't at that stage yet. I think she'd be as embarrassed as you would be."

"My point exactly, and I don't want to create more walls between us."

He looked down at the list she'd given him. He tapped it. "Thank you for this. It's good work. Did you get a grasp on the scheduling program?"

"No problem with that. It's similar to the one I used in Pennsylvania."

Daniel sat back in his chair and studied her for a moment. "I'm glad you're here, Emma. You really are an answer to a prayer."

She didn't know what to say to that. "Thank you," she murmured.

Before their conversation turned even more personal, she said, "I'm going to check over the appointments you've lined up for the week." Without waiting for a reply, she left his office and this time shut the door.

Daniel had spent moments during the afternoon imagining Emma in a bathing suit. When he finished work around five, he wondered if it was too late to join Emma and the girls at the pool. Maybe he'd just drive by and see if he could spot Emma's car.

However, he drove home first. Finding an empty house, he checked on Fiesta, then quickly changed into his bathing suit, stepped into board shorts, slipped on flip flops and grabbed a tank top. He headed out with a towel and his duffel bag. At the pool he wasted no time showing his membership card and entering the pool area. Immediately, he spotted his daughters in the pool. Their suits were neon colors so it wasn't hard to find them. Then he canvassed the area around the pool, and his focus stopped as soon as he spied Emma.

She wore a one-piece turquoise suit with a halter top. Sitting on the blanket, her gaze was turned to the three P's. The sun shining on her hair brought out the red highlights. She was beautiful. What was he thinking, showing up like this? He should have stayed at work or back at the house.

Just then Emma turned, saw him and waved.

Yes, he had been thinking about retreating but now he couldn't. He was already sweating and he was sure that wasn't just from the sun's heat.

It didn't take him long to realize that Emma's gaze was roving over him. Did she get revved up when she looked at him?

The closer he got to her, the more he could see that her cheeks were rosy. Just from the sun? Or from staring at him and maybe having the same thoughts he was having?

He finally stopped at the blanket she'd laid on the grass. He felt an awkwardness between them that hadn't been there before. Deciding there was no point in dancing around the subject, he just came out and said, "You look gorgeous."

Her face expressed surprise. Didn't she know how pretty and sexy she was?

Then he remembered what John had done to her. It had probably been easy for insecurity to set in, easy not to trust a man, easy to see all compliments as idle flattery.

All that meant he'd said the wrong thing.

Pippa and Penny had spotted him now. They were jumping up and down in the pool, shouting and waving.

He waved back and called, "I'll be in soon." He turned back to Emma and asked, "How many times have you slathered them with sunscreen?"

"Three and counting," she answered, looking away from him.

"Do you want me to put my tank on?" he asked her.

That brought her gaze back to his. "No, of course not. You're at the pool."

"We are, but I'm half-naked, and you're looking like a swimsuit cover girl."

"Nonsense," she scolded. "Those girls all wear bikinis or else half their breasts are showing."

Daniel chuckled.

"What?" she asked, indignant.

"Emma, in some ways you are so innocent and in others, you're so honest. I never know what to expect."

"Sometimes you hold in what you're thinking, and sometimes you're straightforward. Are we even?"

He smiled at her. "*Should* I put my tank on? I really don't want you to be uncomfortable."

"No, no tank," she said with some admiration in her voice. "Do you work out?"

"I have weights in the master suite. After Lydia left, I turned her walk-in closet into my weight room."

It was obvious Emma was trying to hide a smile.

"What?" he asked. "In some ways I *have* moved on."

Now she did smile.

He nodded toward the pool. "Do you want to get wet? I know the girls shouldn't stay in too much longer."

"I was thinking the same thing."

Daniel walked close to Emma as they made their way to the pool, but not so close that their arms brushed. He motioned her to go down the steps first, and then he followed. He noticed right away that Paris was swimming laps rather than playing with her sisters or the other kids in the pool. He frowned but decided to talk to her later. She had to learn that exercise in moderation was the best way to go.

Penny and Pippa dog-paddled over to them. "Want to play ball?" Penny asked.

"Only if we don't bother anyone else doing it."

"There's a spot over there," Pippa said, pointing.

Daniel swam to the deep end and retrieved a ball from a net hanging there. When he reached the shallow water again, he tossed the ball and Penny caught it.

It wasn't long before they were all diving under the water for the ball, jumping up to catch it and tossing it again before anybody could catch their breath.

Penny tossed it at Emma. Emma dove but Daniel did, too. They bumped into each other under the water and he grabbed her around the waist. He was holding her as they came up for air.

For that moment, the world stopped spinning. For that moment he didn't feel the coolness of the water against his skin. He only felt heat. He and Emma generated it. She was pressed against him and reflexively his arms brought her closer. They were staring at each other as if there was no other place in the world to look. Emma's lips parted slightly and he practically groaned. He couldn't kiss her, not here, not now, and definitely not in front of his daughters.

Reality must have crashed down on Emma at the same time it crashed down on him. Her legs and arms fluttered as she moved away and out of his grasp.

"Did you trip, Emma, and couldn't find your way back up?" Pippa asked innocently.

Penny added, "Daddy says I'll always float to the top if I relax."

Emma didn't look any more relaxed than he felt. Still, she recovered and told Pippa and Penny, "I found the ball the same time your dad did, and we practically tripped over each other."

The two girls laughed, and Daniel gave Emma credit for telling them the truth without being totally honest… unless she really thought that was all that had happened.

Daniel swam off after that and decided to swim a few laps himself. After his fifth lap, he bobbed up and saw that his daughters and Emma were exiting the pool. The exercise had helped him regain his composure. He supposed he was ready to try to ignore Emma's body in her wet bathing suit as they all prepared to go home.

When they returned to Daniel's house after swimming, Emma watched Paris carefully. She thought Paris had looked pale after she'd gotten out of the pool. She shouldn't *be* pale with the sun they'd had that day. She'd asked Paris if she was feeling okay and Paris, as always, had brushed off her concern. From the first day she'd been here, Emma had taken notice that Paris still wasn't eating as much as her sisters. She'd also witnessed Daniel scolding Paris, encouraging her to eat more. That hadn't helped.

Once they'd changed clothes and Emma had hung up the bathing suits to dry, feeling a bit shy about hanging Daniel's on a drying rack on the screened-in porch, she heard Paris tell Daniel, "I'm going to check on Fiesta."

Emma decided to take the opportunity to talk to Paris. Maybe she could frame it in a way that wouldn't put Paris on the defensive.

A few minutes later, Emma let herself into Fiesta's room and closed the door. She smiled when she saw Paris sitting on the floor, Fiesta nestled in her lap. "She's bonded with you."

Paris looked up at Emma, her hair still wet from her shower. In that moment, she looked much younger than eleven.

"Do you think she's healthy enough to feed her kittens?" Paris asked.

"She's eating much better. If we keep feeding her well while she's nursing, hopefully they'll have enough to drink." Emma took the opportunity to make a comparison. "Fiesta needs the right nutrition, not only to have healthy babies, but to be able to nurse them. That's why we chose the cat food that has the right nutrients."

Paris narrowed her eyes and stared at Emma. "Are you trying to make a point?"

Emma shrugged. "Maybe. Cats and people have many similarities. Just like Fiesta, you need the proper nutrition for your bones to grow and strengthen, for your hair to be glossy, for your skin to have a healthy glow. Exercise alone won't do that. You need vitamin-rich foods, a balance of protein, carbs, fats and fiber."

Emma lowered herself to the floor beside Paris and

began to pet Fiesta. She stayed quiet and Paris didn't ask any more questions. But when Emma finally left the room, Paris appeared to be thoughtful. Thoughtful enough to listen to Emma and her dad?

Emma hoped that was possible.

Knowing they would be spending the afternoon at the pool, Emma had planned for a quick supper—toasted turkey-and-cheese sandwiches along with a salad and the iced tea she'd prepared earlier. It would be an adequate meal. Pippa and Penny would raid the cookie jar. Emma wanted to bake homemade cookies with them tomorrow to have something a little better for them than the store-bought brand.

After dinner, when Paris had only taken two bites of her sandwich and eaten a bowl of salad, Daniel asked Emma, "Do you need help cleaning up?"

"Not tonight. There's not that much to load into the dishwasher. I'm sure you have other things you'd rather be doing."

"I did bring work home, but if you need help, I'm here."

Remembering exactly how she'd felt in Daniel's arms in the pool, she quickly repeated, "I'm fine."

Daniel looked as if he wanted to say something, but then he nodded and headed for his office. By the time Emma returned to her suite, her skin was prickly. Checking the neckline of her sundress, she saw her skin was indeed red against her gold locket. She wore the locket every day because inside of it was a memory of her mother.

Now she unhooked the clasp on the locket and set it on the dresser. She'd been so concerned about the girls slathering on sunscreen that she'd only remembered to do it to herself once. She'd lowered the straps on her sundress and was ready to smooth lotion on her sunburn when Daniel came into her room. She'd absently forgotten to close the door.

Daniel stopped when he saw her before the mirror, her straps lowered. He came closer and she was immobilized. The moment seemed to be electric, pulling them toward each other.

Daniel gently touched her shoulder and ran his fingers down the path of the sunburn on her arm. "That's going to hurt later."

She turned to face him. "It's starting to hurt now," she murmured.

"You felt what happened to me in the pool today," he said. She felt a bit dizzy with Daniel being so close. He'd showered before supper, too, and she caught a whiff of soap—and male.

"What happened?" she asked softly, knowing she was blushing.

Yes, she had felt his arousal. But would that have happened with any woman...or just with her? When Daniel tilted his head, she knew what was coming. She *could* back away and deny the feelings she was starting to have for him.

But she didn't.

She was holding her breath, expecting his lips to find hers, but they didn't. He kissed her cheek first. She'd been kissed on her cheek before, mostly by family. This was totally different. The feel of his lips on her skin created such turmoil inside of her. She wanted more. Yet, she couldn't be impulsive.

But Daniel was kissing her cheek again and then the corner of her lip. All she could do was reach up and encircle him with her arms. She did want more than nibbles. She wanted more than this. To her dismay, she wanted *him*. Their near-tryst—his body intimately pressing against hers—in the swimming pool had shown her that.

It wasn't just his lips on hers that created the need inside of her, it was the scent of him, the tautness of his muscles, the feel of his arms around her. She couldn't think, not about anything in the past, not even about the future. The fire between them in the present was all she could see and hear and feel and give in to.

His arms tightened around her, and she knew she should break away. But his kiss was masterful and exciting and everything she'd ever wanted to feel.

Then a question entered her mind: What did it mean?

That question brought her back down to earth. She pushed away and when she did, her head cleared. Suddenly she heard Daniel's daughters scrambling down the stairs. Pippa's voice was sweet and high. Penny's voice was lower and rambling. Paris's voice was modulated.

Daniel didn't try to keep her in his arms. As soon as she retreated, he did, too. "I don't regret that," he said huskily. "Do you?"

She had to tell him the truth. She shook her head and pulled the straps to her dress back up to her shoulders. "No, I don't regret it. But what does it mean?"

He ran a hand through his hair and looked troubled. "I'm not sure. But the one thing I can tell you is that I haven't felt this attraction to a woman in over two years. I think that says something, don't you? Tell me how you feel."

"I feel lost and confused. I told you that in the past I was impulsive and I don't want to be that way again."

"I understand."

His words were sincere and she believed him.

Daniel nodded to the door. "I can hear the girls. If I can hear them in here, then they're being pretty loud."

Emma smiled. "I guess that means they're either excited about something or angry about something. I just hope Paris isn't angry with me. I thought she looked pale when she got out of the pool, so I spoke with her earlier about the nutrition that Fiesta needs, and how it's not so different from what humans need. I mean, cats need the right nutrition to make their bones grow and their fur glossy, while we need nutrition to be healthy and strong. She seemed to take it in, but I don't know if she's going to take it to heart."

"One other thing that I like very much about you is the way you care."

She had been hoping this attraction wasn't just physical and his words now made her feel lighter, even happier. "I do care about them. I'm just not sure what to do about Paris."

"All we can do is keep them all engaged. If we listen to them, hopefully they'll listen to us."

Did he really mean that?

"I know you probably want to put something on that sunburn," he continued. "I was going to let the girls watch a YouTube video of a cat having babies. Do you want to join us?"

Yes, she very much wanted to join them. However, she feared that every bond she made with Daniel and even his daughters could easily be broken if he decided he didn't want her in his life anymore. She shouldn't get too attached.

She responded to him in the most tactful way. "I think

watching that video would be a special moment for you with the three P's. So I think I'll stay here."

Studying her for a long moment, Daniel said, "Maybe you're right. I'll let you know how it goes in the morning."

"In the morning," she repeated, looking forward to making breakfast for him and the three P's. She wanted to enjoy every minute of being part of this family that she could...before it ended.

Chapter Seven

In his office the following day, Daniel couldn't stop thinking about that kiss with Emma last night. He suspected she didn't just want an affair. What did *he* want? He felt a real need for her. The thing was—was that need only physical?

He was still contemplating that question when the he heard the buzzer from the reception area—probably the woman coming to interview for the associate position. Emma had insisted that today she needed to do chores around the house so he told her he didn't really need her at the office. He'd have to answer the door himself.

When he opened it, he found an attractive woman there. He asked, "Megan Jennings?"

Megan was about five-eight with wavy black hair that hit her shoulder blades. She was pretty, with high cheekbones, full lips and light brown skin.

Her dark brown eyes studied him now, as if she was assessing him. "I'm Megan."

He immediately extended his hand to her. They shook and then he motioned her inside.

Daniel was dressed in a short-sleeved oxford shirt and khaki slacks. Even with the air-conditioning, sometimes the humidity snuck in.

Megan, on the other hand, was wearing a navy blue suit, but there wasn't a bead of sweat on her brow and he had the feeling she was used to wearing suits.

In his office, Daniel had her résumé in front of him on his desk. He'd called her references and they'd been stellar. Tapping the sheet in front of him, he said, "I can't find anything wrong with you!"

She kept a straight face, but he thought he saw the corner of her mouth twitch up.

"What am I supposed to do?" she asked. "Give you a list of my faults?"

"That might be a good start, so I know what to expect."

She seemed unfazed by his humor and his request. Daniel was glad she wasn't easily scared away. That was important.

She responded, "To start with, working in a law office, I believe everything I have to do should be professional."

"No argument there. Why do you think that is a fault?" he asked.

"Some clients might think I'm a little standoffish."

"Good to know. Anything else?"

"I'm single, particular and I'll drop a client if he or she isn't honest with me."

Daniel's gaze met hers. "Right away?"

"That depends. Sometimes people lie because they're

scared. I can understand that. But if they lie more than once, then I know it's a problem."

"You're talking about criminal-defense matters? I didn't think that was your specialty."

"It's not. I guess what I'm saying is that I've dealt with white-collar crimes, too. I've met CEOs who don't think they need to tell the truth to anybody."

"I know what you mean."

"Let *me* ask *you* a question."

"Go ahead." It would be interesting to see what she asked.

"Why are you hiring an associate?"

"I used to have a partner, but he took a position at an Alexandria law firm. Since he left, work has piled up considerably and I need an associate."

"And I need a job," she said honestly.

"I understand you moved here from New York City."

"Yes, I'm a transplant but so excited about the house I'm renting. It's in the historic part of town. I've never lived in a house like that."

Glancing down at her address, Daniel frowned.

"What's wrong?" she asked, apparently reading him correctly.

"I just noticed your address. I have to warn you that you have an eccentric neighbor who's constantly under the threat of eviction. I've never been pulled into the situation directly, so I don't know the details. But I thought you should know."

Megan just shrugged. "If that becomes a problem, I'll take care of it. I've been on my own and I'm used to taking care of myself."

Leaning back in his chair, pleased with the conversation, her résumé and references, he admitted, "Usually in this situation, I would have my office manager show you around, bring you up-to-date on the computer programs and that type of thing. But Raina is out of town for two weeks. My nanny, who has office-manager experience, will be filling in when she can, but she had other things to attend to today. Maybe tomorrow the two of you can get together and she can show you around."

"Does that mean I'm hired?" Megan asked with a sparkle in her eyes.

"That means you're hired," Daniel concluded. He breathed a sigh of relief. Nanny problem solved... Associate problem solved.

This had been a good start to the summer.

However, he thought about that kiss with Emma last night. The situation with her could grow more complicated than he wanted it to be. He'd deal with that when he had to. He'd become good at compartmentalizing. His daughters came first. Work came second. And Emma? In time, he'd figure out where she fit in.

When Daniel came home, Emma was in the backyard with the girls. Pippa, Paris and Penny were playing dodgeball and Emma was strolling up and down the flower bed, looking pensive. The rhododendrons were blooming and she reached out to take one of the blooms in her hand. It was bright fuchsia. As she meandered down the garden along the house, she also stopped where snapdragons bloomed. She apparently liked flowers. Good to know.

Lydia had liked jewelry, not flowers.

The comparison made him want to forget the idea altogether. After he joined Emma by the garden, she looked up and smiled. Her hair had curled in the humidity and she'd tied it back. She looked younger that way.

"How's the sunburn?"

She was wearing a tank and shorts and he could see she was still red.

"It's not as sensitive this morning. I even put sunscreen on before I came out here."

"You were playing dodgeball, too?"

"Until they got the best of me. I'm not very good at pummeling my opponent with the ball."

Daniel laughed. "*You* see it that way. The three P's see it as sports."

"Pippa's not too fond of it, either." She pointed to the youngest, who had headed over to climb the combination jungle gym and treehouse.

As close as he and Emma were standing, their arms brushed when Daniel turned to look at the girls. "I hired Megan Jennings."

"You did? That's wonderful. So she was what you were looking for?"

"Yes. I think she'll work out really well. Do you think you could come in tomorrow while the girls are at camp, show her around and introduce her to the computer programs?"

"Sure."

He glanced at his daughters but then his gaze returned to Emma once more. She was studying him, too. That pull of attraction he couldn't deny was yanking on his emotions...and his regrets.

"Your managerial skills are on the level of a CEO's," he said.

"That's idle flattery," she teased.

"No, it's not. The way you scheduled the three P's and

the way you've taken over Raina's job in the office without blinking an eye… You're talented, Emma Alvarez, whether you want to admit it or not."

She looked speechless for a moment, but then she admitted, "I don't think anyone's ever told me that."

"Then I'm glad I'm the first." His voice had gotten a little husky and he didn't know what that meant. He'd figure that out later, too.

Daniel heard a loud gong sound coming from the house. When they'd moved into this house, he'd learned quickly that the doorbell could be heard in every room.

He checked with Emma. "Are you expecting anyone?"

"No. You aren't?"

"No. Unless Shannon decided to make another unexpected appearance. She often does that. She also knows to come around back, though. I'll go check."

A few moments later, Emma was shocked when she saw who came into the backyard with Daniel. It was her father!

Knowing her mouth had rounded, she quickly closed it. Jorge Alvarez looked as king-like as he always did. When she'd read storybooks with her mom, her father always reminded her of the king…and that's how she thought of him. He was a tall man and his shoulders never slumped. Well, that wasn't quite true. They'd slumped for a while after her mother had died. But then he'd regained his footing and become the father she knew now. And at this moment, he didn't look happy.

"Your father came to visit you," Daniel said nonchalantly, as if it was no big deal. "Though when I told him you were out here with the girls, I could tell that he didn't realize you had a job as a nanny."

Emma gave Daniel a wide-eyed stare that told him the cat was out of the bag, so to speak. Although her father was around teenagers and college-aged students all day, he was still a traditionalist.

Because Daniel had only explained one half of her situation here, and she wanted her father to know she hadn't lied to him, she told him, "When the girls are at their camp, I'm Daniel's office manager."

Her father crossed to her and glanced around the yard. When his focus fell on Daniel's daughters, his expression softened a bit. However, when he returned his attention to Emma, she could easily see that disapproval again.

Her father still had a full head of black hair. He was wearing a short-sleeved white shirt and dress slacks with shiny loafers. Yes, this was her dad, who rarely wore jeans. He thought his students needed to see him at his most professional.

He said to Emma in a terse tone, "Emelina, you're living with a man you hardly know."

Emma put a finger to her lips and nodded to Daniel's daughters. "I have a suite for myself on the first floor. Daniel and his daughters sleep upstairs."

"You have a lock on your door?"

"Yes, I do." But she didn't tell her dad that she hadn't used it.

Her father's wary glance at Daniel told her he still didn't trust him.

Nevertheless, Daniel stepped forward, unwilling to be left out of the conversation. "I have the utmost respect for your daughter, Mr. Alvarez. I would never do anything against her wishes."

Jorge Alvarez still didn't look convinced.

Daniel added, "I'm divorced, with three daughters

who demand all of my attention when I'm not working. I intend to provide a good example for them. Let me introduce you." Daniel put two fingers to his lips—lips that Emma remembered vividly against hers. He whistled.

As soon as Paris, Penny and Pippa heard him, they turned toward him, waved and ran toward the house.

"You have them well trained, Mr. Sutton."

"Not trained," Daniel responded with a smile. "They just know the signal. It helps me call them when they're farther away than my voice. I don't let them out of my sight unless they're with another adult I approve of."

Her father seemed to look at Daniel with renewed interest. "You're a wise man, Mr. Sutton. But as they grow in age, you'll find keeping them in your sight will become harder and harder."

"Dad…" Emma warned.

"Emelina moved to North Carolina without consulting me. I still don't know the whole story."

Emma was grateful when all three girls skidded to a stop in front of them. She explained, "This is my dad."

Pippa was the first to step forward and offer her hand to him. "It's good to meet you, Mr. Alvarez."

Emma saw Daniel try to suppress a grin at his little girl acting so grown up. Before her dad could hide his surprise, Pippa latched onto his hand and asked, "Do you want to see my cat? She's going to have kittens soon."

Paris and Penny both protested. "She's *our* cat."

Pippa was already tugging Emma's father toward the sliding glass doors.

"C'mon. It's cooler inside," Penny added, beckoning to him.

Paris was silent but followed Pippa.

Her father gave Emma a pointed stare, then shrugged. "I suppose I'm going to see a cat."

As soon as they were all inside, the three P's took Emma's dad upstairs.

Daniel placed his hand on Emma's shoulder and she felt warmth—not only there, but also through her whole body. "They'll soften him up."

"Children can do that," Emma commented. "But I'm going to have to tell him about moving to North Carolina because of John. I've never kept things from him before."

"Will you move out if he disapproves?"

"No, I will not move out. I'll be clear that I have my own life and I've had it for years. He treats me as if I'm sixteen when I'm twenty-six. Giving in to him will only reinforce his behavior."

Daniel chuckled. "We'll see what he thinks about that. My guess is, he'll do a background check on me as soon as he can."

"Oh, Daniel. I'm sorry."

When he squeezed her closer, she felt the comfort of his strength. But it was more than that. She *wanted* to be close to him.

"I don't have anything to hide, Emma. A background check doesn't scare me."

"You seem to be taking this unexpected visit in stride." She admired that and the way he'd handled himself around her dad.

"Ever since Lydia left, I've had no choice but to take each curveball as it comes. We'll invite your dad to dinner and Pippa will steal his heart. How much do you want to bet?"

Emma couldn't believe the next few hours passed so quickly. She'd learned her father was staying at a bed-

and-breakfast at the edge of town. He seemed to think Daniel's daughters were worth his time because he regaled them with stories about Emma growing up and the times he spent with his own grandfather, riding on the train and blowing the whistle. Even Paris seemed interested.

After the girls asked to be excused, Daniel and her dad began discussing the economics of the region, the way small towns were being revamped, why Daniel needed to add staff to his law practice. Daniel, of course, didn't go into the whole story, but he did reveal Megan's credentials and said he was looking forward to working with her.

Emma's father glanced at Emma, maybe to see if she minded that Daniel had hired a new woman to work with. She purposely kept her expression blank. She didn't mind. First of all, she had no reason to be jealous. And second...he wasn't the type of man to go around kissing every woman he met. For whatever reason—instinct or women's intuition—she was sure of that.

It wasn't long until her father decided, "I'd better be going. I'm driving back to Pennsylvania in the morning."

Daniel shook his hand. "It was a pleasure to meet you. Can you say goodbye to my daughters before you leave? They enjoyed your stories."

"You've done a fine job of raising them. I can tell."

A few minutes later Emma and her father were standing in the foyer alone. "I'm happy here, Dad."

"You think this is what you want now. Tomorrow or next week might be different. I want you to come home, get an advanced business degree and start a real life."

"My life is real. Penny, Paris and Pippa need me."

"You are *not* their mother. Where is she?"

"She left. Daniel told me she hasn't seen the girls for a very long time. She's written them a few notes, but that's it. They need a woman's guidance."

Her father patted her shoulder. "And what life will you have after you give it? Think about that, Emma, before you decide to stay here permanently."

"Dad—"

He held up his hand to stop her. "Just think about everything I said. Agree to do that."

"I agree," she answered, feeling like the sixteen-year-old who'd been coaxed to make the same comment about curfews and other rules. It was a sign that they were both attempting to be on the same page. However, this time they weren't. Her growing feelings for Daniel changed everything.

After her father left, Daniel came to stand with her in the foyer. "Was that a tough goodbye?"

"Not exactly. He wants what *he* wants for me. I want what I want. But he left on good terms, I think," she said with a weak smile.

Daniel came close enough to her that he could reach out and tuck her curls behind her ear. "What do *you* want?"

"I'm finding out day by day. That's all I can tell you."

After he studied her, he nodded. "Same here. The thing is… I seem to want more each day." He ran his finger along her jawline. "More of *you*."

She felt dizzy from the need she saw in his eyes. She felt as if they were both taking a ride into uncharted territory that could be dangerous. She wouldn't be impulsive. If she thought logically about Daniel, wouldn't that guide her to the right conclusion?

In her mind she saw a conclusion—the two of them

in bed together. Was that what Daniel wanted? Simply that?

Too soon to know. But she'd better find out quickly before it was too late.

Daniel didn't come home for supper the following evening. He'd called and told her he was working late to acquaint Megan with some of his clients and to answer some questions that had cropped up after Emma had given her a preliminary tour that morning. It was easy for her to offer, "I'll prepare a plate for you that you can warm up when you get home."

There was huskiness in his voice when he responded, "Thank you, Emma."

She didn't know why that simple thank-you had touched her like it had. Maybe because it was so heartfelt.

She was hoping she could find time alone with Daniel tonight. Something had happened with Paris when she'd taken the girls clothes shopping that he should know about. The result of that excursion was that Paris was upset.

Daniel arrived home around 7:00 p.m. Penny and Pippa were playing games on the TV. Paris had gone upstairs to her room to read. At least that's what she'd told Emma she was going to do.

Emma sat with Daniel, drinking a cup of coffee as he ate dinner. He told her about a case he was working on. She'd seen the papers on the divorce settlement while she was working in the office that morning.

He explained, "It got more complicated today. Clarice has decided she wants a car *and* the house. Of course, Dave is fighting it. I suggested mediation, so we'll see."

"Do you mind if I ask you a question?"

"I might not be able to answer it, but go ahead and ask." Daniel pushed aside his plate and picked up his glass of sweet tea, taking a few swallows.

Emma watched his large hands hold the glass, studied the hair on his forearms that curled a bit, watched as his throat muscles worked to swallow. *Get a grip*, she told herself. She focused on her question. "Did you and your ex-wife have a problem coming to a settlement?"

Daniel appeared surprised at her question but not disconcerted. "Lydia just wanted out of the marriage. I cared about full custody of the girls. There really wasn't much to settle."

Emma decided they'd better arrive at a nonpersonal footing again. "Would you like anything else to eat?"

"No, I'm good. Emma, you don't have to wait on me. That's not part of your job description."

Feeling a bit embarrassed, she stood. He did, too, then picked up his plate and glass and took them to the sink.

Now was the time to discuss Paris. "Can I talk to you? Let's go to my room," she suggested. "It will be more private."

His gaze was questioning, but he simply said, "Sure."

Daniel followed Emma to her room. She felt nervous about what she had to say. But the conversation couldn't be helped, not if she was really serious about watching over his daughters.

Once in her suite, Daniel went to the love seat.

Emma sat next to him and plunged right in. "I took the girls clothes shopping today."

"O-o-okay," he said, drawing out the word. "Did you spend more than you expected?"

She had spoken to him about shopping ahead of time

and he'd given her cash so she wouldn't have to worry about a credit card.

"No, the money wasn't the problem. We found good sales. Paris—" She stopped and cleared her throat. "Penny and Pippa seemed delighted with what we bought."

"But Paris…?" He wore a worried look now.

"Paris tried on a dress she loved but she couldn't get into it, because it was too tight. She was upset. I told her we'd find something just as cute in her size, but Paris told me she wants to be the size of that dress. I'm concerned the talk we had about healthy eating didn't make a difference."

"That settles it. I'm going to make an appointment with her doctor. Maybe he can talk some sense into her about healthy height and weight for her age. I don't want this to become a worse problem than it is." Focusing on her, he smiled. "Thank you for caring. I know the three P's can feel it. That will make such a difference in their lives."

"They're making a difference in *my* life. You are, too," Emma admitted.

With her admission, he circled her with his arms and pulled her closer. Her lips found his and his found hers. His kiss was passionate and powerful and could lead them right to her bed.

When she pulled away, he let her go. But as he did, his finger caught in the chain of the locket she always wore. He was careful not to break the delicate chain as he leaned away. His voice was a bit deeper than usual when he said, "You wear that locket all the time."

"Except when I'm swimming," she said lightly. She reached behind her neck and opened the clasp. With the locket in her palm, she pressed the little button on the edge and the two sides popped open. Inside was a picture of her mother and father when they were young.

"This belonged to my mother. She told me she put that photo of my dad in there soon after she met him. She was sure he'd be her husband. This locket is probably my most prized possession."

As Daniel studied the photos, Emma thought she heard the tap of shoes on the hardwood floor in the hall outside her doorway. But when she turned to peer out, no one was there. Maybe she'd imagined it. Maybe she just wanted a distraction so she wouldn't end up in Daniel's arms again.

His green eyes darkened and she recognized the desire that told her he wanted to kiss her again, maybe harder and longer this time. However, instead he wrapped his hand around hers, the one holding the locket. "It's good that you have something of your mother's that brings back memories of her."

"That's what my dad said it would do when he gave it to me."

"Then your father is a very wise man."

Daniel was right. Maybe she should consider her father's wisdom more seriously.

Chapter Eight

Emma sat at the reception desk the following morning, very much aware of Daniel in his office. Being distracted by him didn't interfere with her work, but when each task was completed, she thought about him. She thought about how he'd looked in his swim trunks on Monday at the pool. She thought about his scent when he'd kissed her. She thought about his deep voice as she heard him on the phone with clients.

He kept his office door open. Had he done that with Raina, too? Or was this a new habit, for her…in case she needed him?

She thought again about what her father had suggested—that she go back to Pennsylvania, finish her degree, get a real job. All of that might be logical but it didn't sit well in her heart. Whether she did it quickly or took a long time to think about it, she always followed her heart.

When the main line to the office rang, Emma took the call. "Hello, Daniel Sutton's law office."

"You aren't Raina," a woman's high-pitched voice said in complaint.

"No, I'm not Raina. She's away for a while and I'm standing in. But Daniel's here. May I help you?"

"If Daniel's there, that's all right then. We trust him."

Was that the royal *we*? Emma wondered. "May I ask who's calling?"

"Oh, my. Raina knows my voice. You don't. I'm Birdie Whitaker."

"Hello, Miss Whitaker," Emma said. She was definitely familiar with the name because Birdie and her sister, Bunny, were co-owners of Furever Paws Animal Rescue. "I volunteer at Furever Paws. Though we haven't met officially, I know you and your sister do so much to help animals."

"And you must be the young woman who convinced Daniel to take Fiesta home. You're like Bunny. You can't turn an animal away."

Emma smiled. Apparently, Birdie knew exactly what was going on at the shelter. "I'm also Daniel's daughters' nanny. I thought taking in Fiesta would be a good experience for everyone."

"A woman after my own heart. Animals teach children responsibility. You're on the right track there."

Again Emma had to smile.

Birdie went on, "I don't want to take up too much of your time, but my sister and I would like to consult with Daniel about our legal affairs. Would it be possible for Daniel to come out to see us?"

Emma would put Birdie through to Daniel right now

except she heard his voice on the phone and the light for line three was lit.

"Daniel's on another call right now, but I'll check with him and get back to you as soon as I can. Would that be all right?"

"Oh, yes. Bunny and I will be here all day."

"It was nice finally speaking with you, Miss Whitaker."

"You, too, Emma. Maybe you could come along with Daniel. We can talk animals all we want."

Emma laughed out loud. "That sounds good. I'll talk with you soon."

After Emma ended the call, she saw line three was still lit. She inputted notes into the computer and filed papers. When she was finished, she saw that Daniel was off the phone. She went to his door and softly rapped.

He motioned for her to come in. "You don't have to knock."

"It just seems the right thing to do." Her gaze and Daniel's locked for what seemed like an eternity. She remembered the way she'd felt in his arms. Was he remembering their kiss? The way his eyes darkened, she supposed he might be.

"Is there something you needed?" he asked.

"Birdie Whitaker called. She'd like to know if you could come to the estate to consult with her and her sister about their legal affairs."

"That's not a problem," Daniel assured her. "Just find out when she'd like to meet. I have free time this afternoon if that's a possibility." He paused. "Do you know anything about the Whitakers?"

"Only that she and her sister are co-owners of Furever Paws."

"Both sisters are unmarried and they live in their family's original home," he explained.

"Never married?"

With a shrug, Daniel elaborated. "Rumor has it that Bunny was engaged in her twenties, and her fiancé died tragically. But she's always willing to share happy memories. Birdie, on the other hand, never discusses her past relationships."

"So how did Furever Paws come to be?" Emma had never heard the entire history of the shelter.

"Our office has done legal work for them in the past. Their father left the property in equal shares to them and their two brothers. The brothers sold out their shares completely, and over the years the sisters have smartly sold small sections of their property and they live off the investments. But now, theirs is a pocket of undisturbed land with developments going up all around them. They were constantly having stray animals dropped off on their acreage. They started an animal refuge but it became too much for the two of them to handle financially, so they filed for nonprofit status and started the Furever Paws Animal Rescue."

"So they don't have animals on their private property now?"

Daniel smiled. "Oh, yes, they do. Whitaker Acres is home to goats, pigs, geese and I think even a pair of llamas that they took in."

"Do you think they'll sell off more of their land?"

"They've told me more than once they've no intention of selling more land. They want to leave Whitaker Acres as a trust. They're hoping their investments will keep them and the shelter afloat for a long time. But maybe they've had to reevaluate their financial situation. When a tornado came through in March, it caused major damage to the shelter. Birdie and Bunny hadn't realized their insurance had lapsed. The whole town came together and threw a big barbecue cook-off and raised enough funds to fix the damage. I think they've also gotten some financial grants, but maybe the money wasn't enough after all, especially since they used a chunk of it to expand the shelter's capacity. I believe that screened enclosure they're adding for cats will be the last of the changes."

Daniel stood and came around the desk. With him closer now, Emma quit thinking clearly. She knew there was something else she wanted to tell him. It came back to her as he stood in front of her and she looked up at him. "Birdie asked me to come along when you go to the estate so we can talk animals. It's clear she loves pets even though she says that Bunny is the sister who can't turn an animal away."

Daniel's eyes searched her face. She suspected he wanted to touch her, yet he didn't—maybe because they were in his office. His voice was husky as he said, "I have a feeling you can't turn them away either, true?"

"Maybe so," Emma murmured. Before the sparks between them could light into a fire neither of them could put out, she suddenly came up with an idea. "You know I like to volunteer at the shelter. What if I took the three P's along with me? I'm sure there are things they could do there that would help."

"That sounds like a good idea. It would give them a sense of service. I know in high school they have to sign up for service projects. This would be a start."

Neither of them seemed to want to move away, but then suddenly Daniel snapped his fingers. "Something I wanted to tell you. I was on the phone this morning with our family physician. I made an appointment for Paris but the physician who usually sees her is on vacation. The appointment is in two weeks. I thought it was better that Paris felt comfortable with somebody she knew than to make an appointment sooner with a stranger."

"I'm sure you're right about that. Just let me know when it is and I'll put it on the calendar."

Daniel told her the date and time. She gave him a smile and took a step back. "I'd better note this before I forget."

Daniel didn't protest but nodded. "Just let me know when Birdie wants to see me."

"I'll call her back right now," Emma assured him, then left his office before she stayed… Left his office before he could kiss her again… Left his office so she'd remember it was business only when they were there.

Daniel drove Emma to Whitaker Acres. Fortunately, Birdie had wanted to meet at 1:00 p.m. That was great since his girls would still be at their camps. He slowed as he drove toward One Little Creek Road.

"How old is the house?" Emma asked.

"It's one hundred years old. It's a little weathered but well kept. The metal roof helps."

"I like the white clapboards and it has Victorian details."

Daniel pulled up in the parking area beside the house. The front porch was large, with rockers and hanging plants.

"You can tell the sisters really care about this house. Look at those flower boxes."

Emma was speaking of the flower boxes under every

window that were all decorated with burgundy-painted wood shutters.

"I love the etched-glass windows on the wood front door," she added.

Daniel noted another car was parked on the gravel.

After he and Emma climbed from his vehicle, they rounded the house and went up the steps to the porch. Daniel pressed the bell.

The door opened and Daniel said, "Hi, Birdie. This is Emma."

"Oh, yes. I recognize you from the shelter. Bunny's in the parlor. Come on in." Birdie's smile was wide as she ushered them inside. She was tall and thin and in terrific shape for age sixty-four.

Daniel watched Emma as they walked on the plank flooring into the parlor, which was decorated with plenty of chintz as well as flowers and ruffles and elegant doilies. To his surprise, Richard Jackson was sitting there. The local veterinarian with the twinkling light brown eyes was African American and his hair was black with a touch of gray at the temples.

"Doc J," Emma said. "It's so good to see you again."

"You and the doc know each other?" Daniel asked.

"Doc J helps the animals at Furever Paws."

Dr. Jackson stood and came toward Emma. He took her hand and shook it, then did the same with Daniel. "Hello, Daniel. It's been a while."

Daniel realized that in a town as small as Spring Forest, the older residents usually knew all about the younger ones. "It has been a while. How are you?" He knew the doctor's wife had passed away five years ago.

"I'm fine, always good when I'm visiting Birdie and Bunny." He cast his glance at the two of them.

Daniel had heard the rumors that Dr. Jackson was sweet on one of the sisters, but nobody knew which one.

"My daughter, Lauren, is working with me now," the vet explained. "She's going to take over when I retire at the end of the year." He took a step back. "I know Birdie and Bunny have called you in for important business, so I'll leave you to it."

Birdie was quick to protest. "You don't have to go. You know all about most of our business."

The vet chuckled. "Maybe so, but I still think it's best I leave." He turned to Daniel and Emma. "These two lovely ladies took pity on me and invited me to lunch. They fill my social calendar so Lauren believes I have one."

They all smiled and both sisters walked the veterinarian to the door. When they came back in, Birdie sat on the sofa and invited Emma and Daniel to take their seats.

Bunny perched next to her sister and picked up a folder that was on the coffee table. "I know your time is valuable, Daniel, so we'll plunge right in. Birdie has put these notes together so she'll explain why we need you."

Daniel knew Bunny, whose real name was Gwendolyn, was a year younger than Birdie. She was shorter and plumper, too, but still very pretty. Sometimes Daniel thought she was a little naive about the world in general, but she was a great support for her sister and for the shelter.

Emma had taken out a legal pad and pen. "Daniel has asked me to take notes. Do you mind?"

"Of course we don't mind," Bunny assured her, plumping the silver waves over her brow. "And after we're done here I want you to tell me all about Fiesta. Did she have her kittens yet?"

"Not yet," Emma said. "But after we finish business I'll tell you what Daniel's daughters think of her and how we set up a room for her."

Bunny's eyes twinkled. "I look forward to it."

"All right now," Birdie said. Daniel appreciated the fact that Birdie usually spoke her mind. In the long run, that saved time and misunderstandings.

"You know how fond we are of Gator," Bunny began, jumping in ahead of Birdie.

"Now, sister," Birdie gently chastised. "We have to tell Daniel everything." Birdie turned to Daniel. "Our brother is younger than we are but he thinks he knows better than we do. It's because of that investment firm he works at in Durham, North Carolina. There's no denying he's made himself a lot of money, but the truth is if he had common sense, he wouldn't be twice married and twice divorced. He'd be closer to his teenage sons. But that's neither here nor there. He has insisted that our investments are fine, but as you know he let our insurance lapse. That kerfuffle has us worried that he might be letting things slide."

Bunny looked terribly embarrassed as she said, "Birdie thinks there's something wrong with the paperwork, too."

"There's not enough of it," Birdie complained. "We should be getting monthly statements. But anytime I ask Gator about it, he isn't forthcoming."

"What would you like me to do?" Daniel asked.

"We'd like you to investigate all of our legal work. In this folder I have our wills, medical power of attorney and durable power of attorney that you drew up for us. I also have the new insurance papers, which I took care of myself. We'd also like you to investigate our investment accounts. Give us an accounting of what has been taken out, what has been put in and what interest or dividends we have earned. Can you do that?"

Daniel glanced at Emma, and she caught his look. She seemed to understand what he was thinking before he said it. She said, "Will you be asking Megan to assist you?"

He explained to the sisters, "I just hired a new associate, Megan Jennings. She has an accounting background, so if you're comfortable with her being involved, she'd be great at doing a preliminary report for me. I will check over everything and then report back to you. How does that sound?"

"That sounds perfect," Bunny responded with a wide smile. "Now, let's talk about the most important things in life, like animals, while we have tea and cookies. Sound good?"

Daniel knew each of his visits ended with tea and cookies. He didn't dare refuse. When he gave a nod to Emma, she said, "Tea and cookies sound lovely." He liked the way she related to the Whitaker sisters. He liked the way she related to *him*.

Daylight was just crawling between the slats of the blinds when Emma awakened. She felt a gentle hand on her shoulder. Daniel's voice was close down to her ear. "Emma? Are you awake?"

She'd been dreaming about Daniel, and now his deep baritone vibrated through her in a rhythm she was coming to know. She opened her eyes and there he was, hovering above her. His hair was mussed, but his eyes were worried. She couldn't help but see that he wasn't wearing a shirt. She'd felt those hard abs against her when they were swimming. She'd felt *him* against her.

She couldn't believe the thoughts running through her head. She couldn't believe she wanted to pull him down into bed with her. Sometimes she felt crazy when daytime dreams floated through her mind—dreams of princes and princesses and happily-ever-afters. Had he come down here to kiss her and—

"Emma, I think Fiesta needs you. I think she's going to have her kittens."

That statement certainly awakened Emma. She sat up quickly and propped herself up on her elbows. Then she realized her tank top, with its thin spaghetti straps, was dipping lower than it should. She yanked it up and sat up, keeping her shoulders straight. "What's going on?"

"I heard her meowing and I went in to check on her. She's circling the room and climbing in and out of that nest you made for her in the plastic bin. What should we do?"

She liked the fact that he'd used *we*. He felt part of this undertaking, as she did. "Wake the girls. They're not going to want to miss this. We can't all be in the room at the same time, but one of us should sit with her until we know what's going on."

"Even Pippa?"

"Why don't we let Pippa go in first for a short time? You and I will be right outside if she needs us. Do you think Fiesta just started meowing?"

"I think so. I'm a pretty light sleeper. I didn't hear her before now."

"Let's go see what's going on."

The three P's were practically bouncing with excitement even though they'd just awakened. Emma said,

"Too many people in the room could cause a delay with Fiesta birthing the kittens. So each of us will just keep her company for a little while, and we'll take turns."

Daniel gathered his daughters around him. "I need you to calm down if you can. If you're calm, my guess is Fiesta will stay more calm. She's going to want comfort, not excitement." He raised his eyes to Emma's. "Right?"

"Exactly."

Then he explained, "But one of us will be right outside the room if you need us."

They decided that the order of going into the room would be Pippa, then Penny, then Emma, then Paris. Emma could determine what was happening because she'd seen kittens born at the shelter. She'd also watched some YouTube videos with Daniel and his daughters.

When it was Emma's turn to sit with Fiesta, she saw the longing in Paris's eyes. Maybe an exception was in order here. She crooked her finger at Paris and they both went in to Fiesta, who was circling the bin, stepping out and then stepping back in. When she was out of the bin, she would circle the room, rubbing against the condo and anything else that came into her path.

"What's she doing?" Paris asked in a whisper.

"She scenting where she's been. That way when the kittens are old enough to be out and about, they'll know their mother's smell."

"Really?"

"Yes, really. She can set boundaries for them that way."

"I guess it's sort of like me recognizing my mother's perfume when she was around."

This was the first Paris had spoken of her mother.

"Yes, it's the same thing. Or you might be able to tell she's been in a room by the scent of her shampoo."

"With Mom, it was perfume. With you, it's shampoo."

Emma was surprised that Paris had noticed. Then again, preteens could be quite perceptive.

Fiesta came over to Emma for a while and settled in her lap. Emma stroked her patiently and gently, murmuring to her that everything would be all right.

"Do you believe that?" Paris asked.

"I do—why?"

"I hate when people say that and they know it's not true. After Mom left, Dad told us that all the time. And it wasn't true. Nothing was all right for a really long time."

Emma could hear anger in Paris's voice. "Did you ever tell your dad how you felt about it?"

"No."

"Why not?"

"Because Penny and Pippa needed to believe it."

"And you didn't?"

After a long pause, Paris shrugged. "Maybe."

"I think you should tell your dad how you feel. If you're honest with him, maybe he'll be more honest with you."

Fiesta chose that moment to move over into Paris's lap. Emma thought she saw Paris's eyes glisten with tears but she wasn't sure. The comfort of an animal could do that. Or maybe Paris finally letting her feelings off her chest had done it.

Suddenly Fiesta gave a loud meow, stepped over Paris's legs and went into the bin. She circled and then lay down.

"I think it's time," Emma said softly. "If she has more

than one, there could be minutes or even an hour between each one. Hopefully you'll each get to see a birth."

"Are you going to call to Dad?"

"Let's wait and see what happens."

What happened was within minutes Fiesta delivered her firstborn. "I'm going to show you what to do," Emma said. "That way when your dad comes in you can tell him."

"But I don't know…" Paris began.

"Just watch. If she breaks the birthing sac quickly, we don't have to do a thing. But if she doesn't, we have to do it for her."

They watched as Fiesta did break the sac and began washing her newborn.

"She does that for stimulation," Emma told Paris.

"Look, it's yellow and fuzzy. Aw, isn't it cute? It's so small!"

Daniel was in the room when the next kitten was born. Emma had left the door open a few inches so Penny and Pippa could hear what was going on. As Emma had directed, Paris told him exactly what they should do when the second kitten was born.

Paris came out to fetch Penny. "Be really quiet," she told her. "Fiesta and Dad know what to do."

Emma asked, "What color is the second-born?"

"It has yellow and brown and black and white."

It was three hours later when Emma and Pippa saw the third kitten born. It, too, had yellow, brown, white and black, but not as much white as number two. When the three kittens were nursing, Penny asked, "Is she going to have any more?"

"We just have to watch and wait."

Paris said, "Can we go down to the kitchen and get breakfast?"

"Cereal?" Daniel asked. "You can all get that easily enough. I'm going to stay up here with Emma for a little while. Come get me if you need me."

Paris gave her father one of those looks that said he had to be kidding. "I can pour cereal and milk, Dad."

"Of course you can," he said lightly. "And I know you'll watch over your sisters."

"Aw, Dad," they said in unison.

They were standing right outside the door of Fiesta's room and Daniel put his finger to his lips. "Let's keep quiet for a bit so we don't scare Fiesta or the kittens."

The girls went clomping down the stairs while Emma and Daniel returned to the room. "Do you think she'll have more?"

"I don't know. But number three is having trouble latching on. If she won't, we'll have to bottle-feed her."

"Her? How do you know? I mean, it's too soon, isn't it?"

Emma laughed. "It's the coloring. Mostly female cats are that coloring. We really shouldn't handle them too much, but they need to nurse." She gave the third kitten a gentle little push and she finally latched onto her mom's nipple.

As Emma and Daniel sat in the room together on the floor, leaning against the wall, Emma could hardly take her eyes from momma and kittens. Finally, however, she turned to Daniel and said, "Does Paris ever talk to you about her feelings?"

"She hasn't been talking about much at all lately."

"I think she'd like to have some honest conversations with you. Can you be open to that?"

"You mean, conversations where I don't act as if I'm going to judge what she says?"

Emma nodded. "Also, where you tell her the truth about your feelings if she asks. Don't try to sugarcoat anything."

"What did she tell you?"

"I believe she needs to tell you herself."

"Emma, if it's important—" He sounded annoyed with her.

"Everything's important at that age."

Staring at Emma, he nodded. "I guess that's true. What about you? Are you honest with me about your feelings?"

She kept her gaze on the kittens. "I don't know what you mean."

"Sure, you do. What were you thinking when I came to wake you this morning?"

"I…" Emma hesitated. "I don't know."

Daniel shook his head. "Yes, you do. I'm not going to judge what you say because my guess is that we were thinking the same thing."

"All right." If he wanted honesty, she'd give it to him. "I was thinking that if you kissed me again, it might not stop at that."

"Exactly," he agreed. "That's exactly what I was thinking."

When he leaned toward her, she knew he was going to kiss her. She wanted him to. When his lips came down on hers, she kissed him back until somehow she ended up in his lap and he was holding her. Emma didn't know how long the kiss went on. She just knew there was no-where else she'd rather be.

Finally when Daniel raised his head, he gave her a

crooked smile. "We've been trying to deny this but even two of us being in denial didn't help. My feelings for you are growing stronger, and I want you more and more each day."

Emma sighed. "Oh, Daniel. Is this the right time for either of us?" *What if I'm wrong about Daniel, as I was about John?*

Daniel really must be getting to know her well because he said firmly, "I'm not John. I don't have a fiancée in the wings. I would never ever betray a woman that way. I wouldn't betray *you*."

She wanted to believe him. Oh, how she wanted to believe him.

Fiesta meowed and Emma scrambled from Daniel's lap to check on her. "She looks tired and spent."

The birthing of kitten number four was slower than the others. As soon as the kitten was delivered, Fiesta lay still, obviously exhausted.

Emma said, "We need to break the sac. I'll break it and you wipe the kitten with that warm cloth, okay?"

"Okay."

They worked together in stimulating the kitten and helping it breathe. It was all black and fuzzy, and soon started squirming and rooting for its mom's nipple.

They watched to make sure it got attached, then Daniel said, "I'll call the girls. They're going to want to see this."

It was one of those moments that needed an exuberant expression of feeling. Daniel hugged Emma and she hugged him back. They kissed and it was coaxing and gentle and perfect. Then Daniel pulled away and stood. "I'll call the three P's and I'll remind them to be quiet."

Emma knew the girls would have excitement that

would bubble over, too, and that was okay. Hugs all around were called for.

However, fear stole into Emma's heart. She was getting close to Daniel. She loved Daniel, and she was forming bonds with his daughters. What would happen if what they were feeling fell apart?

Chapter Nine

Daniel watched Emma make sure that Fiesta had everything she needed. That included a darkened room and quiet. The problem was... Emma was quiet, too. That meant something was wrong.

The three P's were in their rooms getting dressed. Daniel had decided it was okay if they skipped their camps today to keep checking on Fiesta and the kittens. Emma was watching the momma and babies carefully. She had been concerned until the last placenta had been delivered. However, she still wanted to make sure that Fiesta's birthing was over.

After Daniel jogged down the stairs, he spotted Emma coming his way. She said to him, "Fiesta has food and water. I'd like to feed her every few hours. She needs her strength for nursing."

"I set up the baby monitor."

"I saw the speaker in the kitchen. That will help if we hear anything unusual going on."

Emma wasn't quite meeting his eyes and that wasn't like her at all. "Is something bothering you?" he asked. "Something I said?"

"No, not anything you said. But I have to ask you—do you want me forming bonds with your daughters?"

He wasn't sure how to answer that. All five of them were forming bonds like a family. Would an affair between him and Emma be good for his daughters? What if Emma left?

"I think you're good for them. Paris is especially opening up more around you, and Pippa seems happier than I've seen her in a long while. Penny still likes sports more than anything else. But that's Penny."

"What about *our* bonds?" Emma asked, looking more serious than he'd ever seen her. She must have been doing some hard thinking.

Suddenly he had to tell her the truth, and the whole truth. "If you're asking how far we can go, I don't know. I don't know if I can ever fully trust a woman again."

Emma's face fell. "Maybe I should leave now before the girls get more attached to me."

"Is that what you want?" He looked her over. *Pretty* didn't begin to describe Emma. He was incredibly attracted to her, but the connection growing between them went deeper than that. She had love in her heart to give, but he didn't know if he could accept it. His daughters certainly needed it.

When she didn't answer him, he said, "Tell me something, Emma. It's not that long ago that you found John with his fiancée."

"Almost two months," she said, her chin lifting.

"I just wondered if you're over him…over what you shared. If you loved him, it seems to me you'd still be recovering."

"What are you accusing me of, Daniel? Not caring enough? I thought I loved John. The truth was that I didn't know him. How could I love a man who thought trampling on my heart was easy, who thought having a fiancée in another state was okay? He lied to me, and when I walked in on him and his fiancée, any feelings I had for him died. Except maybe anger. But I learned long ago that anger isn't productive. That would only hurt *me*, not *him*. So I began volunteering. A coworker told me about a studio apartment I could rent month-to-month, and I started over. That's what I'd wanted all along, only this time I decided I didn't need a man by my side to do it."

He believed her. "I don't want you to leave."

She shook her head. "But if there's no chance that you can have real feelings for me, I don't know if I should stay." A strained silence settled between them. Finally she asked, "Are you going in to work today?"

"Yes. I called Megan and told her I'd be late. I gave her a key when I hired her. I have to start looking into the Whitaker sisters' affairs. Megan can handle the financial aspect, but I want to do a little snooping around of my own. Bunny and Birdie might love their brother Gator, but I'm not so sure he isn't trying to pull a fast one on them."

Daniel had pulled on a T-shirt with his jogging pants, but now he had to change into his office clothes. "If anything happens and you need me, you know you can call me. I'll try to come home early, but then I'll have to go into work again tomorrow."

She nodded then turned toward the kitchen. "I'll see what I can round up for lunch." She was gone before they could add to or finish their conversation.

Except what was there to finish?

He'd turned toward the stairway when he heard a rustling up above. By the time he reached the first step, he didn't see Penny, Pippa or Paris there. Had one of them overheard his conversation with Emma? He hoped not, because his daughters' world was unsettled enough.

Emma didn't know where else to look. Her locket was missing.

Daniel *had* come home early and checked on the kittens and his daughters, who were sitting quietly by the side of the box watching them. Emma had come to her room to change for the evening. As she'd taken off her blouse in favor of a tank top, she'd realized she wasn't wearing her locket.

After checking the dresser, the drawers in the dresser and every spot she could get to in her room, she still couldn't find it.

Hurrying to the main part of the house, she practically ran into Daniel. Holding her by the shoulders, he took one look at her and asked, "What's wrong?"

"I can't find my locket." Her voice was a bit wobbly.

"Emma, it will be all right. We'll find it. We'll ask the girls to help. When did you last see it?"

That was a logical question. "Last night before I went to bed. I took it off as I always do at night. I laid it on the dresser."

"You're sure?"

"Yes. I always spread out the chain so it doesn't tangle. That's the last I saw it. Today when you woke me, I didn't even think about putting it on. We were busy with the kittens and Fiesta all day. I changed my blouse just now and realized I wasn't wearing it. But when I checked the dresser, it wasn't there. Daniel…" She knew there was a pleading note in her tone, and she didn't know what to do about it. That locket meant so much to her. It was the only connection to her mother that she still had.

Daniel brought her close for a hug. He murmured beside her ear, "I know what that locket means to you. Let me call the girls. We'll all look for it."

An hour later, all of them had searched for the locket but none of them had found it. They had each taken a room and then traded with someone else. When they gathered in the family room once more, Daniel told the three P's, "I want to remind you that this isn't a lost trinket. This locket belonged to Emma's mother. Even though her mom died, it still gives her a feeling of connection. I know it seems we looked into every nook and cranny in this house, but we're going to do it again. This time I'll go with you room by room and I'll move the furniture while you look. Does everyone understand the new plan?"

Paris, Penny and Pippa all nodded.

Emma simply felt like crying. They were doing their best for her. However, this might be a hopeless cause.

Another hour later, they all joined up in the kitchen.

Daniel put his arm around Emma's shoulders, and she was surprised by the gesture in front of his girls. He saw her surprise and explained to his daughters, "Emma has become important to us. We care about her, and we want to find that locket. I doubt if the locket got dragged outside, but we have daylight left. Let's take a walk around the house and along the woods. If we don't find it now and it's out there, maybe tomorrow we'll find it when the sun glints on it."

"We should check on Fiesta and the kittens," Emma reminded him.

"I was just up there. All four kittens are nursing and they'll go to sleep after that. I'm sure Fiesta needs a rest, too. So we're good for a little while there. When we come back, we'll check again."

Logical, Emma thought. Daniel was so logical. The facts mattered to him, as they would to any lawyer. Yet when she looked into his eyes, she saw more than logic. He did care about her, and each day she was falling more and more in love with him.

Love. When had *that* happened? Maybe if she kept her mind on finding the locket, she wouldn't be so scared by the idea of loving Daniel.

Outside, Pippa stooped over as if she'd found something in the grass. But when she picked up the object, it was just a white stone. Paris thought she'd found something but it was just a seed pod from a sugar gum. Not to be outdone by her sisters, Penny searched long and hard, examining the yard as if it was a grid. But all she came up with was a penny.

When they began to walk along the woods, Emma knew they wouldn't find the locket tonight, not out here. Daniel soon slowed his long-legged strides so that his daughters and Emma could keep up. He mostly walked beside her, their shoulders brushing, neither of them moving away. His daughters didn't seem to notice as they skipped and jogged in front of them, carefree as only children could be.

Daniel said in a low voice to Emma, "I know nothing can replace that locket."

"I still have the memory of it," Emma said. "My dad still has photos of him and Mom. I can buy another locket and put one of those pictures in it."

"You're a brave woman, Emma Alvarez, but you don't have to pretend with me. I know you're feeling devastated. I would be, too. Let's give it a few days, though, before you give up hope. It could be in that one place we didn't look."

"Thank you," Emma said.

He leaned away. "What for?"

"For being you."

When he smiled at her, her heart seemed as buoyant as a balloon. Maybe they still *could* find the locket.

Suddenly Pippa called, "Dad, come here. There's a dog. Look."

Penny pointed, too. "He's darting in and out."

It was almost dusk and Daniel tried to see what they were seeing.

Paris explained, "He's small and gray and really scruffy. He was over there by that tree."

Daniel put his finger to his lips, directing his daughters to be quiet. After he crouched down, he whistled softly.

The dog peered at him around the tree.

"Come here, boy," Daniel coaxed. "We won't hurt you. Come on."

But quick as lightning, the dog shot into the woods.

"I'll see if I can find him, but you all stay here."

The girls gathered around Emma and she circled them with her arms. She didn't merely feel like a friend to them. She felt like a mom. The feeling totally caught her off guard.

When Daniel returned to them, he was frowning. His

shirt was torn and his arms were scratched from either thorny bushes or tree branches.

"I couldn't find him. My guess is he knows the best hiding places in these woods."

"We can't just leave him out here," Pippa said, almost near tears.

"Honey, we have no choice," Daniel told her firmly. "But I'll tell you what. We'll put out a bowl of food and a bowl of water on the porch. If he comes around and eats, we'll be helping to take care of him. And if he keeps coming around, we'll try to catch him. Okay with you?"

Somehow Daniel had again found a solution so that his daughters wouldn't worry quite as much. Emma tapped his arm. "We should go back to the house and take care of those scratches."

He gave a shrug. "They'll heal."

"With some antiseptic and antibiotic ointment," Emma pointed out. "Right, girls?"

"You should listen to Emma," Penny told her father.

Although he grumbled about it, Daniel finally nodded. "I'll listen to Emma after we put food out for the dog."

Emma considered ministering to Daniel something to look forward to.

After they returned inside, Daniel found two burgers in the refrigerator that they chopped up and put in a bowl. Pippa watched while Emma filled a water bowl. They all went out to the porch and set the bowls near the edge.

Daniel gave Pippa a huge hug. "Dogs have great noses. If he smells food out here, I'm sure he'll come over and eat it."

"But it doesn't have ketchup or mustard on it," Pippa complained.

Daniel could see that Emma was trying hard to hide a smile and so was he. "Honey," he said, "dogs can't have ketchup or mustard on their food. It would make them sick. He'll like it plain, I promise."

"And now I have to take care of your dad's scratches and cuts. Some of them are hard to get to. Can you and Paris and Penny go upstairs and check Fiesta and the kittens, then get ready for bed?"

Daniel knew he was going to hear complaints about that. He added, "After you're all dressed and you've brushed your teeth, you can check the porch to see if the food's still there, okay?"

There were nods all around as Pippa, Penny and Paris went inside.

Daniel insisted, "Really, I'm fine."

But Emma was having none of that. She said, "Some of those scratches are on the back of your arms, and I wouldn't be surprised if you have them on your back, too. Treating those by yourself wouldn't be easy. So let me take care of it, okay?"

He wasn't so sure it was okay, not with the way he felt whenever she was within a few feet of him. However, he didn't want to push it.

They easily heard the girls laughing and talking as they went into the downstairs bathroom. Daniel lifted his shirt over his head and tossed it on the vanity.

He'd shown Emma where all the first-aid supplies were kept when she'd come on board. He didn't say a word as she pulled out bandages, peroxide and antibiotic ointment from the cupboard.

"Are you going to wrap me up like a mummy?"

She laughed. "No. But I even have skin-sensitive bandages here. Penny tells me they're the best ones you've ever used."

He groaned. "Now nine-year-olds are making product decisions."

Emma pulled out the stool under the vanity. "Sit," she ordered.

The bathroom wasn't small, but it wasn't large, either. He was so aware of every move Emma made—from reaching into the cupboard for the bandages, to turning the sink on and wetting a clean washcloth.

To keep himself distracted, he asked, "What's the procedure going to be?"

"The same as for your daughters. We wash the scratches with a mild soap and water and dab them with peroxide, we dry them, then I put antibiotic ointment on the bandage and attach it."

"Why on the bandage and not on the cut?"

"When you put it on the cut, sometimes the bandage won't stick. Believe me, this works best."

"Oh, I believe you," he murmured.

Emma began with Daniel's back, which was probably a good thing because he couldn't see her. However, when she leaned over him to wash the scratches, he could feel her hair on his neck. He began to sweat. "It's hot in here," he mumbled.

"That's just because you're nervous about this hurting."

"I can handle pain," he answered gruffly. "I was eight when I broke my arm. Didn't shed a tear. I was ten when a baseball hit me in the eye. No tears that time, either. I was sixteen when I got tackled until I saw stars. No tears then, either. So don't expect any now."

"Keep talking," she encouraged him. "That will help."

"Only the worst ones need a bandage," he advised her.

"You're the patient. You don't get to say."

Her voice was a little teasing and he almost turned around right then and there to kiss her. He took a deep breath instead.

In the next moment, every scratch on his back stung as she applied the peroxide. He didn't even wince. That stinging was just another distraction, thank goodness. He'd concentrate on that.

However, when she attached the bandages, her fingers smoothing them over his skin, he almost jumped up and said, "Stop." But he didn't. He tried to just take it all in and enjoy the touch of her hand. How long had it been since he'd been touched with caring by a woman? Until this moment, he hadn't realized how much he'd missed it. Nevertheless, he had to put a stop to this, didn't he?

Emma came around his side to tend to his arm. There was a long scratch there that was worse than most of the others. He really should let her take care of that one.

But as Emma washed it, her dark brown eyes met his. He felt as if the pull between them was absolutely right. How could something that felt like this be wrong?

Noticing the pulse at her throat seemed to be beating as fast as his, he asked, "What are you feeling right now?"

She hesitated and then tried to smile. "I'm your nurse. I'm not supposed to be feeling anything."

"From the look in your eyes, I can tell that you are. We have to be honest about this, Emma."

She finished washing the large cut, rinsed the washcloth under the spigot and then did it again. "Let me bandage this one before we try to talk."

As soon as the bandage was attached, he took her into

his arms and pulled her down onto his lap. She didn't try to get away. She looked up at him and he saw there exactly what he was feeling—desire, hunger and possibly more. All of it was happening so fast.

When he kissed her, there was no more pain. There was only exquisite pleasure. The shoulder of her tank top slipped off and he ran his hand across her breast. She moaned and pushed into his hand. That was when he knew he wanted to go further.

But further was impossible. First he heard footsteps, more than one pair, then he heard laughter. Finally he heard Pippa call, "Dad, let's take a look at the porch."

Quickly, Emma scrambled off his lap. They were both breathing hard. "To be continued," Daniel promised.

Emma didn't have time to respond as the door to the bathroom flew open and Pippa ran in. His youngest stopped short and noted, "Emma put bandages all over you."

"Not *all* over," Daniel corrected.

Emma turned away from him quickly, but in the mirror he saw her blush. She was even prettier after having just been kissed, with that pink blush on her cheeks.

He imagined they could both use a cold shower but instead he beckoned to his daughter. "Come on. Let's go see if the pooch visited us."

To Emma he said, "The rest of the scratches will be fine. I'll take care of them before I go to bed."

She just nodded. As he and Pippa left the bathroom, he heard the spigot go on again. He suspected Emma was washing her face with cold water. He wished he could do the same. But when his daughters called, he put them first...always.

* * *

It had been an eventful day in so many ways. Emma was beyond tired. She'd just gone to her room to get ready for bed when there were three knocks on her door. Three?

When she went to answer the door, she found what she'd expected—Pippa, Penny and Paris. "Aren't you supposed to be in bed?" she asked with a smile.

"We are, usually," Penny said.

"But we took a vote," Paris added.

Pippa looked as if she was bubbling with excitement.

"A vote about what?"

"We want to name the kittens. Dad's upstairs with them now. Will you come? You have to help, too. We found *you* when we found Fiesta."

Emma wasn't sure she liked the comparison, but she understood the logic. "Your dad's sure he wants to do this tonight?" He had to be as tired as she was.

Penny leaned into Emma's room. "We didn't give him a choice. We said we weren't going to bed until we named them."

Emma couldn't keep a wide smile in check. She supposed if Daniel ordered them to bed, they would go. But for something this exciting, and to help them with the disappointment after the gray dog hadn't come back for the food, Daniel was allowing them to stay up a little longer.

"All right. Let's go."

The three P's ran ahead of her down the hall. Emma had to jog a little to keep up. On the way up the stairs, she called to them, "Have you thought of any names?"

"Nothing we like," Paris called back.

Daniel was sitting on the floor, his legs crossed, staring at the little bundles of fur. A few days ago, he'd plugged in a night-light and that was on now. It was in the shape of a hot-air balloon with a basket that lit up. It must have belonged to one of his daughters.

Emma lowered herself onto the floor beside him. Her leg brushed his knee, but she didn't move away. They'd gone beyond that.

"When will their eyes open?" Pippa whispered.

"At about ten days," Emma responded. "They'll have blue eyes for a while but then they'll change."

"Into gold and green?" Penny asked.

"Maybe a combination of the two."

"So what are you thinking of naming them?" Daniel asked.

They all sat in quiet for a few moments. Emma could hear the beating of her heart and was aware of Daniel beside her. Was his heart beating as hard as hers?

Finally Daniel offered, "The yellow one could be easy. What if we call him Nacho? You know, corn chips with cheese on them? He's those colors."

"That's really fitting," Emma murmured. "What do you think, girls?"

"I like nachos," Pippa declared.

"It doesn't matter if you like nachos," Penny said. "It's whether or not the kitten reminds you of one."

"He sort of looks like a nacho, only he's furry," Pippa agreed. Daniel tried to suppress a chuckle but couldn't completely. Emma knew how he was feeling. His daughters made the world bright and shiny all over again every day.

Emma asked Paris, "What do you think?"

Paris nodded. "Yeah, I like it. You know the other

ones are going to be harder. We don't want something boring like Ebony for the black one."

"Since the yellow one is Nacho," Penny said, "how about Burrito for the black one? He or she is all wrapped in black. When will we know if it's a girl or a boy?"

"The vet will tell us for sure when we take them in for their first shots."

"First shots?" Daniel asked.

"They'll need two distemper and one rabies shot, spaced out, of course."

"Of course," Daniel grumbled.

Paris patted his shoulder. "It's just like taking us for a wellness exam and our vaccines."

When Daniel glanced at his daughter, he seemed to be happy she'd contributed. "That's a good way to look at it."

"The other two look alike," Pippa commented.

The other two kittens had beautiful white chests, white around their mouths and their eyes with tan on their cheeks, and burnt brown on the top of their heads.

Emma pointed to the one who had finished nursing and was curled up under her mom's face. "That one has a brown patch on her head." She pointed to the other one, who was lying tummy-up right against her momma. "But this one has that nacho coloring on her cheeks."

"She does," Paris said. "Why don't we call one Guacamole and the other Tamale? They're both mixtures, and those two foods have all kinds of colors in them."

"We all have to agree," Daniel warned them. "I don't want to hear arguments about this tomorrow."

All three girls held their hands out in front of them

then laid them one on top of the other. Then they lifted them high.

"We won't high-five so we won't disturb them," Penny said.

Daniel smiled at his daughter. "Fiesta now has her four kittens named—Tamale, Nacho, Guacamole and Burrito."

"Pur-r-r-fect," Emma said, drawing out the word so the girls would know exactly what she meant.

They laughed and Daniel shushed them. The momma cat moved restlessly. "Okay, time for bed. Get settled in and I'll be in to kiss you all good-night."

After Penny, Pippa and Paris left the room, Emma just sat quietly next to Daniel, studying the adorable kittens, each no bigger than her palm. "We should weigh them each day to make sure they're gaining weight," Emma said. "There's a food weight scale in the cupboard. That should do for now."

"We shouldn't use it for food anymore, then, so after we're done with it, I'll donate it to Furever Paws."

Emma turned to look at him. Mostly she just saw his profile in shadow. The ambient light backlit his shoulders...very broad shoulders.

She asked, "Do you really mind having Fiesta and her kittens here?"

He gazed down at them and then shook his head. "No, I don't mind. The girls are learning so much—about caring, about responsibility, and about nurturing. Fiesta and her kittens are teaching them that."

"You are, too."

Daniel put his arm around Emma and drew her close. She leaned against him for a few minutes, both of them just enjoying the mood in the room and their growing feelings for each other.

"There's an adoption event at the shelter on Sunday," Emma commented. "Do you want to go?"

"Only if you promise me we won't come home with a dog this time."

She chuckled. "I promise. Once these little ones are scrambling out of the bin, they'll need all our energy to play with them and care for them."

Daniel leaned his head against hers, and then he cupped her chin and turned her face toward him. When he kissed her, she thought a kiss had never been so sweet.

He didn't take it deeper, and instead moved away. "I have to say good-night to my daughters," he murmured.

After a last look at the momma and kittens, Emma rose to her feet. "Sunday after church we can decide what time we want to go to Furever Paws. The adoption event runs into the evening. From what I understand, there will be craft stands and food stands, too."

"It should be fun." Daniel rose to his feet and walked with her to the door. At the top of the stairs they parted.

Suddenly, Emma realized she hadn't felt this happy in a very long time.

Chapter Ten

The adoption event at Furever Paws seemed to bring out half of the residents of Spring Forest. At least, that's what Daniel thought as they arrived and parked amidst the long line of cars that were lined up along the road. The usual parking lot at Furever Paws was part of the production for adoption day. Instead of having dogs in cages, they were arranged according to size in pens—adequate pens that let them roam around and play. Volunteers would alternate walking each dog in the pen. The cats were in cages closer to the shelter walls under the overhang.

Because today wasn't just about pets, crafters had set up their stands on the outer perimeter of the parking lot. Canopies covered most of them for shade. As Daniel and the three P's and Emma entered the area, Daniel asked, "Craft and eatery stands first or animals first?"

"I'm hungry," Pippa announced.

Penny agreed. "Me, too."

"Corn dogs, burgers or chili?"

Penny and Pippa said in unison, "Corn dogs."

Paris said, "Salad," in a low grumbly voice.

Daniel was about to say she should eat something else when he saw the look Emma gave him. He should find another solution rather than scolding. He pointed to a food truck farther away. "There's a taco stand. You liked the tacos we had the other night. I bet if you ask, they'd give you lettuce and tomatoes in a bowl. What do you think?"

Paris gave him a reluctant smile. "It will work. While we eat, you and Emma can roam around the craft stands, then we can all go look at the animals."

Daniel quirked an eyebrow. "Aren't *we* supposed to eat, too?"

Paris blushed. "I guess you can eat while you're looking at the other craft stands. There are signs on all the food vendors not to feed the animals."

"I'm sure volunteers will be watching for that," Emma said. She looked at Daniel. "What are you hungry for?"

He almost said, "You," but instead replied, "Lady's choice."

"I'd like a chili burger."

"A woman after my own heart. I'll order two of those while you look around."

After Daniel scored two burgers, he found Emma at a vintage glassware stand.

"Aren't these beautiful?" Emma asked, pointing to a flower made of vintage glass. He saw it rested on a pole you could stick into the ground. "This would look amazing near your front door."

The flower was made up of a deviled-egg dish in

white with gold trim, a blue flat plate in front of that and a smaller yellow dessert dish as the center of the flower. It was cleverly arranged.

He pointed to a birdbath fashioned of vintage vases and crystal dishes. A small bluebird sat on the top. There were solar lanterns and turtles and mushrooms all made from vintage glassware. "Let's come back to this stand before we leave. You can help me pick out something for the front yard."

With a scanning glance of the parking lot, he saw that the three P's had joined together and were sitting on a bench closest to one of the dog pens. Daniel drew Emma to a bench under the overhang of the building. He could see his girls from here, yet they could have their own sense of independence.

When he opened the bag and produced two burgers, he handed one to Emma. Then he also pulled two soda cans from the bag. "Not that I'm an advocate of sodas, but I thought these would be good on a hot day."

After a long look at his daughters, Emma smiled. "They're drinking soda, too. Did you tell them they could go on a sugar high today?"

He laughed. "Just wait until they pull you to the home-made doughnut stand."

Knowing the day could be hot, Emma had pulled her hair into a low ponytail. She appeared younger—so vulnerable, so pretty, so touchable. He pushed away those thoughts.

As she unwrapped her burger, she said wryly, "If I make a big mess of this, don't laugh."

He produced napkins from the bag. Taking one in hand, he opened it and tucked it into the neckline of her tank top. His fingers brushed her skin. She was eminently touchable.

She gazed at him with that sparkle in her eyes that told him they were on the verge of something good. When he pulled back his hand, she took a bite of her burger. Some of the chili fell onto the foil wrapping.

"Good first bite," he joked.

"Your turn," she teased with a wink. After he took a successful bite, she commented, "I should applaud."

"Or maybe—" he began.

All of a sudden Rebekah came around the corner of the building. When she spotted them, she headed their way.

"Uh-oh," Emma said. "That's her I-want-to-tell-you-something face."

"I certainly hope she's not going to ask you to take another pregnant cat."

Emma playfully bumped his knee with hers. He liked that. He liked the camaraderie between them as well as the chemistry.

"Just the two people I want to see," Rebekah said.

"Any particular reason?" Daniel asked, wondering what the shelter director had on her mind.

Rebekah sighed. "I just felt I need to tell you that there's a bit of gossip going around."

"About the Whitakers?" Daniel asked.

"No," Rebekah said. She leaned down closer to the two of them. "About you…about Emma staying at your house."

"What's wrong with Emma staying at my house? She's my nanny."

"That's what I've explained to anyone who's made a comment, but I just thought you should know. Not that you have to do anything about it. It's *your* life, and you're not doing anything wrong."

When Daniel turned toward Emma, he saw that she'd gone paler. However, she said to Rebekah, "Thanks for telling us."

After Rebekah said she'd see them later, she headed toward the door of the shelter. Emma was silent.

"Tell me what you're thinking."

"I'm not sure, exactly. If my father heard that gossip, he'd be so disappointed in me. He'd tell me I should move out for propriety's sake."

Daniel swallowed hard. "Is that what you want to do?"

Emma looked him straight in the eyes. Then she leaned closer to him and slowly shook her head. "No, that's not what I want to do. I want to stay with you and your girls and keep on doing what we're doing."

"Growing closer?" he asked huskily.

"Yes."

They were still gazing into each other's eyes when they were suddenly accosted by the three P's.

Pippa pulled on Daniel's hand. "You've got to see this schnauzer. He's so cute—cream all over with big brown eyes."

Penny said, "My favorite's the cocker spaniel. She's got that golden blond hair and she has big brown eyes, too."

Daniel gave a resigned sigh. "You realize, don't you, that we cannot take home a dog?"

The three P's all exchanged glances. "Maybe not today," Paris said. "But that doesn't mean we can't sometime in the future. You always say, Dad, anything's a possibility."

His eldest daughter was an expert at throwing his

own words back at him. "Yes, I have said that, haven't I?" Standing, he held his hand out to Emma to help her up. "Let's look at the dogs and the cats. But we're *not* taking any home."

"Not today," Pippa said forcefully.

He knew what that meant. She had her eye on a pup.

Daniel just shook his head as they all walked toward the first pen.

In spite of himself, Daniel had enjoyed the adoption event. Maybe he *was* an animal person. The three P's had left the event with a friend and her parents, eager to go swimming in their pool.

When they got home, Emma went into the family room. He followed her and said, "I've known Cindy's parents since Paris was in kindergarten. They'll watch the girls carefully and make sure they're safe."

The house was awfully quiet, devoid of his daughters' laughter and chatter. At the moment, the contrast felt pleasant. The truth was that he relished time alone with Emma, if that's what she wanted, too.

They'd been standing across the room from each other, and now Daniel approached Emma. "Do you want this evening as time off?"

Tentatively, she nodded. "Sure. I know you have things you probably want to do."

He took that as an opening for an alternative. "We could play croquet or take a drive. Maybe go to a movie."

"Paris told me you like thrillers."

"And I know *you* like romantic comedies. If we stay here with tall glasses of iced tea, we could probably watch one of each. The three P's probably won't be back until bedtime."

"That sounds good," she assured him. "After running after the girls all week, it's a pleasure just to sit and do nothing. You can pick out the movie you want first. I'll go get the glasses of iced tea."

The camps, Paris's swim-team practice and even their volunteer work must have made Emma feel like a chauffeur. Daniel watched her leave the room. That was just like her—she always thought of him or his daughters before herself. He'd seen that over and over again, even with Fiesta and the kittens.

After she returned to the room with iced tea and set the glasses on coasters, she motioned upstairs. "I'm going to take Fiesta a bit of food and check on the kittens."

He wasn't surprised. He knew she loved just sitting there watching the kittens with their mom. "I'll come with you." He enjoyed watching Emma watching the kittens.

After they entered what he now thought of as Fiesta's room, Emma took the momma cat her food and then removed the scale from the closet. Together, he and Emma weighed the kittens to make sure they were gaining weight.

While Fiesta ate, Daniel operated the scale. Emma took Nacho out of the bin first to weigh him. "Another ounce," she said. "He's doing great. I can't wait until they're big enough to play with."

Emma had taught Daniel and the three P's that the least amount of handling at this age was the best. So she was the official handler. Fiesta knew her scent and didn't mind it on her kittens. They weighed Guacamole, Tamale and Burrito in turn. Burrito, the little black one, meowed the whole time.

"I don't hear them meow much," Daniel said.

"Only when they're taken from their mom."

Daniel immediately thought of Pippa and how she'd

cried every night after Lydia had left. He watched Emma handle the fuzzy kittens so carefully, as if each would break. From his experience as a single dad, he knew children had to be handled that carefully, too.

After they'd finished in Fiesta's room, they stepped into the hall and closed the door. Emma pointed out, "It won't be long until the kittens are tumbling out of that bin. We should probably set up a little obstacle course for them that they can run over and jump down. If you have any spare throw pillows, they would work…or maybe a low step stool."

"I'm sure the three P's would like to collect that stuff and would have innovative ideas of their own."

"I'm sure," Emma returned with a grin.

Emma's smile always took his breath away. Sure, she was pretty, but it was her absolute enjoyment of life that drew him to her.

Settling his hands on her shoulders, he said, "Listen."

She cocked her head. "I don't hear anything."

"I know. It's the sound of silence and we're alone. I'd like to kiss you without interruption."

She tilted her head up and her brown eyes held amusement, as well as something else—something much deeper. "You have my permission."

Daniel felt as if he'd just been handed an early birthday gift. He expected the kiss to be pleasurable, as all of their kisses had been. He expected it to be exciting and that's what he was looking forward to so much. But he hadn't expected to get totally lost in Emma— the softness of her cheek against his thumb, the flowery scent of her shampoo and the heat of her body against his. He also hadn't expected the explosion of desire. He wasn't a teenager anymore but he sure felt like one.

The fire that burned in his belly could engulf him and he wouldn't be able to stop it.

He was about to break the kiss when Emma's fingers caressed his neck and slid up into his hair. His anticipation and need ramped up until he could only make the kiss deeper, wetter, longer.

He tried to make his mind work, to brush away the sensuality of the moment, to think about the future. But the future seemed so far away. Still…he caught a thought. He couldn't take advantage of Emma. They were alone and taking the next step would be an easy action to take. But was carrying this further the right thing to do?

He pushed himself to break the kiss. "Emma," he breathed. "We have to stop if we're going to."

She looked up at him as if she was a bit dazed, too. "What if I don't want to stop?"

"I think you should take a minute at least to think about it."

The amusement was back in her eyes as she asked, "Do you want me to count off the seconds?"

He blew out a breath. "Sometimes you're exasperating."

"And sometimes you overthink things. I'm here with you, Daniel, because I want to be. I know you have a conscience to guide you and that you want to do what's right. This feels perfectly right to me. What about you?"

"You've got to be sure."

"I *am* sure."

With that declaration he scooped her up into his arms. "My bedroom's right down the hall."

Emma felt Daniel's desire in every step and in every breath. After he carried her into his bedroom, he kissed her again.

She was hardly aware of her surroundings—the huge king-size bed with its black-and-gray coverlet, the heavy pine furniture, the scarcity of knickknacks except photographs of his daughters. When he sat her along the side of the bed, he asked, "Are you on birth control?"

She nodded. Her ob-gyn had suggested a three-year implant the previous year. She hadn't had it removed yet.

Daniel took her into his arms and held her close.

She sensed he was hesitating and she wondered why. "What's wrong, Daniel?"

"You make me feel like a caveman, and all I want to do is ravage you in that bed. But I also want to make sure this isn't a rebound effect."

In that moment, Emma realized how much damage his ex-wife had done when she'd left with his partner. She'd shaken his trust in the fact that someone could care for him...could love him. And Emma did. But she also knew it was too soon to tell him that—that he might not believe her.

So instead she said, "No rebound effect, Daniel. I promise you that."

Her reassurance seemed to be all he needed to escape the bonds of the past. He undressed her slowly until she was standing before him naked. To her surprise, she didn't feel embarrassed. Instead, she felt proud that he wanted her. She had no doubt that he cared for her. But she didn't know how deep that caring went. It might just take time for both of them to know.

She said playfully, "It's *your* turn now."

He didn't hesitate to let her tug his shirt over his head. He quickly removed the rest of his clothes. They stood before each other, smiling, then embraced and began kissing all over again. The kissing took them into the bed.

In bed, they held each other. Daniel touched her face, her neck, her shoulders. As he did, she snuggled closer to him, their lower bodies almost joined but not quite yet.

"I can't believe how good this feels," Daniel murmured.

"Believe it." She dragged her fingers down his back.

"I need you now."

Emma understood and her surrender to him was so sweet she felt dizzy from it. He kept kissing her and soon he rolled her on top of him, enhancing their pleasure, anticipating their climax.

When he entered Emma, she held on to Daniel for all she was worth. She'd never, ever experienced anything like this before. To her amazement they both found sublime pleasure at the same time. They seemed to be so in sync. She really didn't know where she left off and he began.

In the afterglow, they lay side by side.

Daniel brushed her curls behind her ear. "I'm so glad you're here."

She was glad she was here, too. Nevertheless, in this act of love, she'd realized just how deeply she *did* love Daniel. What if he still didn't really trust her and the future she dreamed of? What if the future she dreamed of wasn't a possibility?

On Monday, Emma picked up the girls from their camps and came home to check on Fiesta and the kittens. She couldn't stop thinking about last evening and how wonderful it had been. Making love with Daniel couldn't be compared to anything else she'd ever experienced. She was so in love with him.

The three P's chatted as they all left again to volunteer at Furever Paws. Daniel was going to meet them there after work.

Today, under the watchful eye of a volunteer, the girls played with the puppies. Several dogs had been adopted over the weekend but a beagle remained, along with a Jack Russell terrier. Emma helped the shelter by cleaning out cages in the quarantine area as well as giving those animals some attention. Time passed quickly and before long, Daniel arrived.

Emma said to the girls, "Let's wash up before we go home."

Daniel's house was beginning to feel like home. She went on, "I made a casserole we can pop in the oven but I'm open to suggestions." She winked at Daniel.

He grinned back and she saw that look in his eyes that meant he couldn't wait to kiss her. "I could be talked into takeout."

Penny and Pippa yelled, "Pizza!"

Daniel studied them and Paris. He said, "Only if we add boneless chicken wings and a salad to go with it."

With a nod from Paris, he decided, "I'll call in the order and head out to pick it up. I'll meet you at home."

As he left, he brushed by Emma and gave her arm a squeeze. She wasn't sure when they'd have time alone again, but she was sure that they would.

Emma reached the house first. She asked the three P's, "Do you want supper inside or on the screened-in porch? We can set the table before your dad gets here." The temperature was in the high eighties but there was a nice breeze going.

"Let's go to the porch," Paris said, and Penny and Pippa agreed. All three helped her carry plates, silverware and napkins out to the table.

Always practical, Penny said, "We usually use paper plates and cups when we eat out here."

"We'll get some the next time we go to the store," Emma promised.

A short time later, Emma heard Daniel's car in the driveway. Within minutes, he'd come through the house and found them. She'd already poured glasses of sweet tea.

Daniel set the food on the table. "A pizza picnic. That's a great idea."

Daniel had ordered two large pizzas. Each was split down the middle with two different toppings—pepperoni, ground beef, extra cheese and broccoli. He said to Paris, "I'll get the pizza cutter."

Emma added, "I'll get the tongs for the salad. Be right back."

Once inside the kitchen, Daniel hardly waited until they'd stopped walking. He took Emma into his arms and began a kiss that was soft and coaxing at first, but quickly turned into passionate and powerful.

When they leaned away from each other, he smiled. "I couldn't wait to do that."

"I couldn't wait for you to do that."

"One more before somebody comes looking for us."

The second kiss took all the power and passion from the first one and escalated it. The pure chemistry between them almost made Emma melt into him. Had this hungry passion been dormant all her life? Had this true chemistry just been waiting for the right man to unlock it? She didn't anticipate what they were going to do next but sank into desire. Need drove them both.

A burst of laughter came from the patio and Daniel ended the kiss. She knew he'd always do what was best for his daughters, and that's the way it should be. He rested his forehead against hers for a moment as if to say he didn't want to end anything at all. Then he murmured, "I'd better get that pizza cutter."

As Emma went to the drawer to find the salad tongs, she wondered what would happen after Daniel's daughters went to bed tonight. Would he come to her?

Before they went outside, he whispered in her ear, "Later."

She'd be counting the hours until they could really be together again.

Daniel was passing around second slices of pizza—except for Paris, who was eating salad and a small bite of the pizza topped with broccoli—when they all heard a car pull into the driveway. Daniel had left the garage door open when he'd put his car in, and the sound carried.

He looked at Emma. "Are you expecting anyone?"

"Not unless my father decided to make another surprise visit."

Pippa smiled widely. She'd really enjoyed the company of Emma's father.

When the doorbell rang, Daniel said, "I'll get it."

Daniel was gone so long that Emma wondered if there was a problem. Maybe with one of his clients? She stayed with the girls in case that was the situation.

Pippa pushed her plate back from the edge of the table. "I'm done." She had tomato sauce ringing her mouth.

Penny nodded. "Me, too."

Emma pushed the boneless chicken wings toward Paris. "One more?"

Paris gave her a look, but she took another and had eaten it by the time they heard footsteps in the kitchen. Daniel appeared with a pretty woman by his side. She was saying to him, "You changed the security code. I couldn't get in with my key."

Her key.

Pippa turned in her chair and almost knocked it over when she flew out of it and ran to the woman beside Daniel. "Mommy," she called.

Lydia stooped to gather her child into her arms.

Penny was a little more sedate as she pushed back her chair and went to her mother. "Are you here to stay?"

"We'll talk about that," Lydia said with a sly smile.

Paris didn't go to her mom. She glanced over her shoulder at Lydia, then turned back around and took a sip of her iced tea.

There was authority in Daniel's voice when he said, "Paris, aren't you going to say hello to your mom?"

Paris didn't turn around. "Hello, Mom."

Daniel's frown was deep but Emma had no idea what he was thinking.

Lydia didn't force Paris to deal with her. Instead she just turned to Emma. "And who is this?"

Daniel's gaze met Emma's, and he seemed to be at a loss for words.

However, Pippa explained easily, "She's our nanny, and the best one we've ever had."

Lydia patted her youngest daughter on the head. "Maybe you won't need a nanny now that I'm here."

This time Daniel spoke up firmly. "Emma and the girls have bonded. There's no reason to disrupt their routine because you came to visit."

"Maybe more than a visit," Lydia reminded him.

It was clear Daniel hadn't expected his ex-wife. It was clear Lydia intended to try to take over. It was clear that they were all in for a lot of trouble.

Chapter Eleven

Emma was reaching across the bed in the guest room, spreading clean sheets, when Daniel came in.

He asked, "What are you doing?"

"I'm freshening the room. I wouldn't want Lydia to think I wasn't doing my job."

"Emma—" Daniel's voice was heavy with frustration. "Did you invite her here?"

He went over to the other side of the bed to help her attach the bottom sheet. It was a bit of a chore on a high mattress, but she could have done it herself. For some reason she didn't want his help right now.

"You have to understand that I've always encouraged her to come back for a visit to see our daughters. They need that."

Emma finished with her side and crossed her arms. "They need a mother who's *here*."

Daniel finished with his side and studied Emma. "Of

course they do. But that's not going to happen. Lydia is married now, living with the man she gave up everything for."

Emma asked, "Everything?"

"Yes. Me, her daughters and our life here."

To Emma's dismay, Daniel sounded as if it had happened yesterday.

Crossing to the dresser, Emma took a pretty pinstriped white-and-lilac sheet from the drawer. At the edge of the bed, she flipped it over the entire mattress. The stripe matched the fitted sheet on the bottom.

Daniel caught the sheet and pulled it to where it belonged.

"Tell me what happened," Emma said, thinking about her and Daniel making love...and realizing now that she might not have a future with Daniel and his daughters.

Daniel glanced at the bed and she wondered if he was thinking about the time they'd spent together. As he sat down on the edge of the bed, he motioned to her.

She sat beside him but their bodies weren't touching. Right now, she just felt betrayed. She tried telling herself that wasn't Daniel's fault. He was correct. His ex-wife had the right to visit her daughters whenever she wanted.

"I have sole custody. The settlement was written up so that Lydia had liberal visitation rights. For instance, if she wants to take the girls to Alexandria, she'd have to get permission from me to take them out of North Carolina."

"And you'd let her?"

"She's their mother, Emma."

Emma was silent until Daniel covered her hand with his. "I worked through bitterness and resentment, telling myself I had to do that for Penny, Pippa and Paris. I didn't want them to be estranged from Lydia even though that's what ended up happening."

"That was *her* fault."

"Yes, it was. But I came to understand that what happened between us had been brewing for a long time."

"What had been brewing?" she prompted, wondering just how vulnerable Daniel might become with her.

"The fact that we had different values and different goals and different parenting techniques had begun undermining our marriage since Paris was born. But the biggest problem between us was the fact that Lydia had always had expectations of me and I guess I had expectations of her, too."

"Can you explain?" Emma requested.

Daniel glanced at the door. "Are you sure you want to do this now? We could be interrupted at any time."

"That's always going to be true."

Studying Emma, and perceptive enough to see that she needed answers now, he agreed. "Yes, I suppose it is." After a pause, he went on. "When I met Lydia, we were on the same campus. I was in law school and she was taking courses in broadcasting."

Broadcasting meant that Lydia had wanted a career in on-air journalism. "She wanted to be an anchor on a TV show?"

"She did, but...we fell in love, or lust, or something. I was ready to settle down. Lydia had always been a daddy's girl. She had a trust fund. I, of course, wanted to move back to Spring Forest because my roots were here. I'd lost my dad my senior year in high school. I lost my mom my first year of law school. My parents weren't in Spring Forest any more but my sister was, along with everyone else I knew here. I wanted to raise a family here. I thought Lydia accepted that. Maybe I needed a family so badly that I overlooked basic differences between me and Lydia. From about the second year of our marriage, she wanted me to get a job in a big law firm in Raleigh or even DC or New York. I'd had a couple of offers. Maybe if I'd taken one of those positions, we'd still be together. I don't know."

Emma thought about that. "Even if you had different goals?"

"Once our kids came along, my goal was making the best life I could for them."

"And Lydia didn't share that same goal?"

"She did, but she only wanted two children. That's what we planned. But life doesn't always go as we expect. Pippa was one of those surprise babies."

"She didn't want Pippa?" Emma couldn't imagine not wanting that bright-eyed, sweet little girl.

"She settled into the pregnancy and she seemed happy when Pippa was born. But afterward—" Daniel shook his head. "Lydia did love Pippa, Paris and Penny, but she and my partner, Allen, fell in love. They'd been having an affair about six months before he and I were offered the jobs in Virginia. She wanted me to take it. I wouldn't. Allen did, and that seemed to be the last straw for her."

Emma already saw Lydia as a spoiled princess— someone who hadn't had to really work for anything she wanted. Maybe this estimation would change while she was around her, but Emma doubted it.

"You didn't have a clue that she was cheating on you?"

Daniel raked his hand through his hair. "I should have. I knew Allen was seeing someone but not who. We were both working on that case that drew national attention. We had press to deal with, we were keeping very late hours. I was away from the house more than I was here. The girls had Lydia so I thought everything was all right at home. After all, once the case was finished we could go back to a more normalized schedule. But by then it was too late."

"I'm sorry, Daniel. I am so sorry."

He shook his head. "I can't imagine why she came to visit now, but I'm sure I'll find out."

"She wants you back." Emma had already figured that out from Lydia's comments.

"She's married to Allen," Daniel protested.

"That might not matter."

"It matters to me. Lydia and I are finished. I don't want her back."

Emma tossed out the one conclusion that mattered. "But your daughters might."

Daniel wrapped his arm around Emma. "That's something we'll have to figure out. Lydia doesn't do anything without a motive behind it. I just need to find out why she's here. At the same time, I want to encourage her to get close to Pippa and Penny and Paris once more."

"But won't they feel abandoned when she leaves again?"

"That's a situation we're going to have to resolve. I'm determined that Lydia won't leave again until we've figured it out."

Emma wanted to ask where *she* fit in, but she was afraid to ask *that* question.

Emma preferred to believe that Daniel no longer had feelings for his ex-wife. However, Lydia was beautiful… down to the manicured tips of her fingernails. The following morning, Emma made breakfast for everyone, although Lydia was late coming downstairs. She was pleasant enough with Daniel and his daughters. Penny and Pippa seemed to have accepted her back into the family easily. Paris, though, was back to acting sullen and quiet.

When Emma took her seat at the table, Lydia turned to Daniel. "I guess she eats with you, too?"

Daniel looked as if a thundercloud had just passed over his brow. "Of course Emma eats with us. She's not a maid, Lydia. In fact—" He stopped, gazed at Emma and then explained, "She's very special to all of us."

Emma had wanted to hear him say "She belongs here as much as you do," but, of course, he didn't want to start a fight and have bad feelings swirling around his daughters. She understood that. But it was hard sitting at the table feeling like an outsider, when a day ago she'd felt as if she belonged. Lydia monopolized the conversation and ignored Emma the best she could.

Emma told herself this was only temporary. To her dismay, she realized she didn't know that for sure.

Daniel suggested, "Lydia, you can stay here with the girls and then drive them to camp. Emma could continue her work in my office without chauffeuring them."

This time Lydia did look at Emma. "I'm sure she gets paid for chauffeuring. And really, Daniel, I need at least a day to acclimate, don't you think? I'm tired from the traffic and the drive. I just need to relax today. Besides, I don't want to mess up your normal schedule."

What Emma was thinking couldn't be said with minors in the room. It was easy to see that Lydia wanted what Lydia wanted, with no thought as to what was best for everyone else. But would Daniel fall into the trap of giving it to her?

To her surprise, Paris spoke up. "Are you all coming to my swim meet tomorrow evening? My times have been really good."

"We wouldn't miss it," Daniel assured her.

"I mean I want everyone there. Even if Mom comes, I want Emma there, too."

Emma reached out and covered Paris's hand with her own. "If you want me there, I'll be glad to come."

Lydia stared at the comfort Emma was giving Paris, and she turned away. Didn't she realize that someone had to give compassion, assurance and confidence to her daughters? What could possibly make her think that she could drop into their lives again and act as if nothing had happened?

Lydia had gone upstairs to get changed while the girls checked on Fiesta and the kittens. Daniel came up behind Emma in the kitchen. He settled his arm around her waist and turned her toward him. "I know you have a lot of questions and things you might want to say but you aren't saying them, to keep the peace."

Emma felt tears come to her eyes...because he understood. "I would never do anything to hurt Paris, Pippa or Penny."

"I know that. I need answers from Lydia. We're going to have to have a discussion so I can find out why she's really here."

"I still believe she's here to reunite with *you*."

He was already shaking his head.

"Maybe she's realized she shouldn't have left in the first place," Emma pointed out.

Daniel stared out the window for a moment and Emma wondered if he was imagining what his life would be like if Lydia hadn't left.

When he turned back to Emma, he asked, "Do you want me to stay until you leave to take the girls to camp?"

Yes, that's exactly what Emma wanted. But she was an adult. She could handle herself in this situation. She'd just focus on Daniel's daughters.

Some mornings Emma walked with Daniel into the garage to see him off. That way he could steal a kiss. But this morning he didn't suggest it. And when he gave her a hug before moving away from her, she could feel the tension in his body. Ever since they'd made love, she could sense so much more about him, about her and about them together. But what if being together wasn't a possibility? Even if he and Lydia didn't reconcile that didn't mean that his ex-wife's presence wouldn't come between her and Daniel.

Emma was clearing the dishes from the table when she heard a cell phone ring. The girls didn't have phones. She exited the kitchen and saw Penny, Paris and Pippa in the family room. She heard a woman's voice, talking low, coming from Daniel's office.

So Lydia felt comfortable going in there? Maybe she simply wanted privacy.

Emma stepped a little closer to the office, knowing she should simply back away. Snippets of the conversation floated out to her. It didn't take her long to realize that Lydia was talking to a friend. Maybe a friend in Spring Forest.

"I'm glad you contacted me. Maybe we can have lunch while I'm here."

There was a pause. "I can be honest with you, can't I, Connie? No, this isn't a vacation."

Emma couldn't make herself move from Daniel's office door.

"I should have never left Daniel. My marriage is on the skids, and Allen can't understand that I still have ties in Spring Forest…like you and Ted. Allen thinks I should have broken off all contact with everyone here."

Her friend must have made a suggestion because Lydia said, "I suppose it's possible he's jealous of Daniel. I don't know what I'm going to do. I'll see what kind of tone Daniel sets. If he gets at all romantic, then maybe I'll come back to him. But even if he doesn't, I want to reconnect with Penny, Pippa and Paris. They've had one nanny after another, and I'm getting the impression that they need me."

It was true that Lydia's daughters needed a mother. Emma backed away from the door. Returning to the kitchen, she didn't know if she should tell Daniel about that conversation or not. She didn't want to keep secrets from him. On the other hand, when he was around Lydia, he might feel differently than when he was just talking about her with Emma. Maybe in Lydia's presence he *would* have romantic feelings. Wouldn't that be good to know?

Emma would just have to go with her instincts and hope they'd lead her in the right direction.

After dinner, Emma went to her room. It had become a ritual to search for her locket every morning and every evening after dinner. She hadn't found it and neither had anybody else. She knew the three P's had searched, too, because Penny had told her they had.

The girls were upstairs with the kittens and Fiesta. They giggled and laughed when the little fur balls moved around their mom—circling, nursing, snuggling in. In some ways watching them made Emma grateful that she'd had her mom as long as she had. In other ways she realized now the missing would never end, just as love never ended.

She was searching in one of the dresser drawers in case the locket had fallen in there when Lydia appeared at the door of her room. Startled by her presence, Emma closed the drawer and straightened.

Lydia studied Emma for a moment and then asked, "Can I come in?"

Emma nodded, not knowing what to expect.

Lydia scanned the room. "I'd forgotten how nice this is."

Being tactful, Emma said, "It's very comfortable."

"So comfortable you don't want to leave?" Lydia inquired.

Lydia looked self-possessed and confident, but Emma could see something in her eyes that said she was anything but. Lydia was short and slender, and moved like a dancer. Her professionally styled blunt-cut hair slid along her cheeks as she walked. There was never a hair out of place, not even in the morning before breakfast.

Daniel's ex-wife sank down onto the love seat. "You know, I really did come back here for my girls."

Keeping silent, Emma waited. She was afraid if she tried to respond, she'd say something she shouldn't.

"You're judging me," Lydia accused.

Deciding to be honest, Emma responded, "I'm trying not to."

"You're *so* wholesome. No wonder Daniel's falling for you. But wholesome gets boring."

"And what are you, Lydia?" Emma kept her tone calm and even. "You left your husband and daughters, and you hardly ever contact them."

"You're so righteous, just like so many other people in Spring Forest. I never belonged here in the first place. I had other interests and other goals. Daniel never understood that."

"Do you really want to talk to me about your marriage?"

After another glance around the room, focusing on the nightgown that Emma had laid out on the bed, Lydia let out a sigh. "No, I don't. But I do want to get closer to my daughters again. You seem to have done that. What's your secret?"

"I don't have a secret. I just care about them. They've probably changed since you left. You need to get to know them again…the way they are now."

"I try to start conversations, but Paris especially just sits there silent. Penny does that, too, sometimes. Pippa's the only one who has welcomed me back with open arms."

"Have you talked to Daniel about them?"

"We'll just get into an argument," Lydia complained.

"He understands them better than anyone," Emma countered. "He's tried to be both mother and father to them."

"Until you came along?" There was resentment in Lydia's words that she couldn't hide.

"I've only known Daniel and the girls a few weeks. You spent years with them. If you brush away the debris from the last two years, you should be able to reconnect. You know them, Lydia. Do things with them. While they're concentrating on something else, they might talk to you."

"All of them? Including Daniel?" That question had a note of challenge in it.

"Daniel will make his own choices. But I will tell you one thing—he will always put his daughters first."

"Do you think I don't know that? It's one of the reasons I left. Daniel had expectations. He believed I should think about the girls all the time, not go to the gym when the girls were sick. I should volunteer at school instead of playing a round of golf. And then when Daniel could have taken a job in Alexandria, a town near DC with all types of cultural events and history and excitement, he turned it down!"

Emma couldn't decide if she wanted to hear about Daniel's marriage to Lydia or not. In one way it was enlightening. In another she felt like a voyeur.

"So you're living in Alexandria now, married to a man that you told Daniel you were totally in love with." Emma did want to get the main facts straight.

"You two have talked about me?" Daniel's ex sounded indignant.

"Sharing feelings and backgrounds is part of being friends."

"The men in my life have never done well when I shared feelings. I wanted a different type of marriage than Daniel did. After Penny was born—" She stopped. Then she went on. "Paris was the perfect baby, content and happy. Even as a toddler, she was easy. But Penny... She had colic for six months. Daniel was at work all the time. He didn't have to deal with the crying. She was a terror at two. Then I found myself pregnant with Pippa. I love her dearly. But three of them was too much."

Emma wondered if postpartum depression had played a role in Lydia's actions. But that was then. This was now. She took a leap into a place where she didn't belong. "Do you want Daniel back?"

If Lydia had been lost in memories and regrets, she pushed them away quickly. "Would you move out if I said I did?"

The word came out of Emma without any hesitation. "No."

Lydia scowled as if she'd expected Emma to turn tail and run. "You might want to rethink that."

"Did going after what you wanted make you happy?" Emma asked.

"For a short time, it did," Lydia replied defensively.

"Before you shake up Daniel's life again, maybe you should figure out exactly what it is you want. Daniel is the same man he was two years ago, only stronger. If you came back, what makes you think anything would be different this time around?"

Lydia stood, her face reddening. "You don't understand at all. Allen sold me on life with him. He said he wanted me and we'd have a wonderful life in Alexandria. But now we argue all the time. He wants me to get a job so I'm not lonely when he comes home late."

"Maybe you could talk about compromise."

"Compromise? All that means is that I'm supposed to give in. You've got to remember, these are lawyers we're talking about. They don't know *how* to give in."

Emma didn't believe that was true about Daniel. On the other hand, did she really know? Yes, she did. He had changed his mind about taking in Fiesta because the girls wanted her so badly.

"You just wait until Daniel decides his latest client or Spring Forest or Penny's recent soccer game is more important than anything else—is more important than *you*. Then you'll look at him differently."

With that, Lydia fled the room. Emma wasn't sure

what had just happened. Did Lydia consider her a confidante or an enemy?

While Emma thought about that, she continued to look in her dresser drawers for her locket. She was unprepared when Daniel marched in looking troubled. "What did you say to Lydia?"

"We talked about several things—why?"

"Because she's upset. She's practically in tears. Penny saw that—and saw that it happened after she came out of here. I really don't need you to stir up even more turmoil right now."

Emma's back straightened. "Lydia came to *me*, Daniel. I didn't go to her. She asked me questions. She told me things I might not even want to know. And then you claim that *I* upset *her*?"

Daniel wiped his hand over his face. "We both might want her to leave, but on the other hand, if her visit can help the three P's in any way, I want her to stay as long as she has to in order to connect with them again. I thought you understood that."

Emma studied Daniel and saw the anguish on his face. She remembered making love with him, the new things she'd experienced, the new things she thought *he'd* experienced.

Her heart felt as if it was weighed down with a concrete block. "You're having regrets, aren't you? You're considering what you could have done differently so that Lydia wouldn't have left in the first place. Old feelings are stirring again. You're wondering if Lydia's marriage to Allen was a mistake and she's realizing it."

Daniel's eyes were stormy and he didn't deny anything she said. "Maybe some of that is true." He came closer to Emma. "But my marriage to Lydia was over two years ago. Of course, I have doubts about my life choices, don't you? What about John? Do you wish that had never happened? Or are you stronger because of it?"

Emma was confused, that was for sure. Could she regret her past and still step into the future? Could Daniel? Was he denying feelings he should look at more carefully? Was she?

Lydia's visit had definitely stirred up a hornet's nest. Emma felt as if she and Daniel had been stung by those hornets already. Maybe the best thing she could do was leave.

Chapter Twelve

Emma knew the girls would be wondering where she was. Needing time to herself, she'd stayed in her room for a little while. But she wanted to prepare a pasta salad for lunch tomorrow. She couldn't hide forever... and she wouldn't.

To her dismay, everyone was in the kitchen. She didn't let that deter her.

She'd cooked the pasta and poured dressing on it earlier. Paris liked cucumbers so Emma took several from the refrigerator and set them on the counter. Then she pulled a cutting board from the bottom cupboard.

"Cooking at night?" Lydia asked.

Emma didn't know if that was an observation or a criticism. She took it as an observation. "Pasta salad is great for lunch after it has chilled overnight so the flavors can blend. Daniel can take some along to work if he wants." She cut him a glance.

He looked back at her with a troubled expression. Because of their argument? Or because of Lydia?

As Emma skinned and chopped up the cucumber, Penny went to her dad. "Can we please take a walk around the woods to look for that gray dog?"

Emma guessed she'd come into the kitchen while they'd been in the middle of a conversation.

"I don't know, honey. It will be dark in about half an hour."

"So we should go right now," Penny insisted. She looked at her mother. "Can you walk with us? Dad won't let us go alone."

Lydia seemed to consider what Penny had said. "I'm not a fan of hiking in the woods."

Then Lydia's gaze met Emma's. She added, "But it would be nice to do something with all of you. As long as we stay on the path, I guess it would be all right. Daniel, are you sure you don't want to come along to protect us?"

"You don't need me along."

"What if we see the dog?" Lydia asked.

"We couldn't coax him out of the woods but if you do see him, you could put food and water out on the porch for him again."

Lydia wrinkled her nose as if that wasn't an attractive prospect, either. What *did* the woman like? Emma knew she liked golf. What else? Maybe tennis. It was possible Paris might like to learn. If she had a chance, she'd suggest it to Lydia, who seemed like she was willing to make the effort to do activities with her daughters.

Penny, Pippa and Paris were ready to go. They led the way to the screened-in porch with Lydia following them.

After they left, there was nothing but silence between her and Daniel. Emma pulled the bowl of pasta from the refrigerator and dumped in the cucumbers. Then she pulled out the basket of cherry tomatoes. She'd halve them, add them to the bowl and stir it all up, then toss in tuna.

"Why didn't you go along?" Emma finally asked.

"Because Lydia came here to reconnect with her daughters. She doesn't need me along to do that."

"So you don't want to spend time in her company?"

Daniel slid back his chair and stood.

Emma could sense him coming closer. When he put his hands on her shoulders, she set down her knife, dried her hands and turned toward him.

"Look, Emma. I said things before I probably shouldn't have. In fact, I should have insisted Lydia stay at a hotel or a bed-and-breakfast. But that didn't seem practical if she wanted to share breakfast with us and put the girls to bed."

Emma had considered Lydia insecure, but now she realized *she* was, too. "You didn't want Lydia to stay here for *you*?"

"If it was up to me, I'd give you the upstairs bedroom next to mine and Lydia the downstairs suite. But I didn't want anything to be too obvious to the girls. At least, not yet. You have to stop imagining that I want Lydia back. I don't." He ran his thumb down Emma's cheek.

Emma lightened her tone. "And why would you want my bedroom next to yours?"

He wiggled his eyebrows. "So that you could sneak in and out."

Something about what he'd said concerned Emma greatly. She wasn't sure why he wanted to hide their relationship from his daughters. It was all so confusing with Lydia here—

Daniel cupped Emma's face between his palms, angled his head and set his lips on hers. Just before he closed his eyes, she'd seen the fire there. That fire caused an ache inside of her. He wanted her. She could tell that from his kiss. She wanted him.

He trailed kisses down her neck, then took his hands from her face and edged them under her shirt. "Let's go to your bedroom, Emma."

"But they could come back," she breathed.

"If the girls are looking for that dog, they'll take their time out there. Don't you want to steal minutes while we can?"

Minutes. Did she want to steal minutes? Yes, she did, even if that's all they were going to have. She wasn't being impulsive. She saw the situation for what it was. She was still making a choice to be with Daniel.

Suddenly Daniel stopped, lifted his head and scanned her face. "What do you want, Emma? I'm not going to try to convince you to do something you don't want. This has to be a mutual decision."

The air in the room seemed to thin. She was making a conscious choice, not because she was so logical, but because she was in love. She loved the outdoor scent that hung around Daniel tonight. She loved the way his eyes twinkled when he smiled. She shivered when they turned a darker green as they were doing now.

She wrapped her arms around his neck and drew him closer. "I know what I want. I want you."

His lips crushed hers as his fingers wove into her hair and his tongue slid into her mouth. The chemistry between them was always explosive, never more than it was right now. In some ways, she felt they were doing something forbidden that made it even more exciting. In other ways...she just wanted to be loved by him.

They kissed the whole way to her bedroom. Once inside, he closed and locked the door. As he turned to look at her, he asked, "Do you want me to undress you? Or should we just get rid of our clothes?"

She smiled coyly because she felt flirty with Daniel, romantic, braver than she'd ever felt before. "I think we better just shuck our clothes because we don't know how much time we have."

They ended up undressing quickly, helping each other. But the helping was teasing foreplay and they both knew it. They tumbled onto the bed like two teenagers who couldn't wait to make out.

Each of Daniel's touches was sensual but tender, too. When he slid his hands over her breasts, she felt as if she might come apart. Pleasure with Daniel was like learning a new word. She'd never exactly known what pleasure was before. Now she did, and she hungered for more of it. Daniel was so much more experienced than she was. She could tell by the way he touched her, as if he knew exactly what gave her the most pleasure. When he dragged his fingers over her stomach, she raised her knees, practically begging him to take her.

"We don't have as much time as I'd like," he murmured. "Are you sure you're ready?"

"I'm more than ready. You, Daniel Sutton, turn me on."

"And you, Emma Alvarez, make me forget what universe I live in." He rose above her and slowly lowered his body to hers.

She passed her hands up and down his arms and then around to his back. With a groan, he entered her. He thrust slowly at first and then faster and faster. She urged him on by rocking her body against his, by scraping her nails down his back, by whispering his name. There was a raw need in both of them. She met his and he met hers. His kiss seemed to penetrate to her soul. This was the man she wanted to hold on to for a lifetime.

The fireworks that happened when they climaxed blotted out every concern, every question and every doubt.

When they'd both caught their breath, Daniel touched his forehead to hers. "I don't want to leave this bed, but we'd better get dressed. If they have to knock on a locked door, Lydia will know what we've been doing."

"Do you care if she knows?"

Daniel rolled to his side and then sat up on the edge of the bed. "It's not that. I just don't want any more conflict or tension. Knowing Lydia, she'll soon tire of being with us and she'll return to Virginia."

"Did she tell you that she and Allen are having problems?"

Daniel looked surprised as he reached for his jeans. "No, she didn't. She confided that to you?"

"I overheard her on the phone with a friend. She said her marriage was on the skids. When we talked, she told me her marriage to him wasn't what she expected. He wants her to get a job. She doesn't want to."

Daniel finished dressing. "If that's true, she might be here longer than I expected."

"And if she is?"

"We'll deal with it, Emma."

She could easily see that Daniel wasn't ready to make any type of commitment to *her*. And once again, after the glorious experience of making love, they were discussing Lydia.

* * *

Daniel and Emma had just dressed and gone into the kitchen when they heard loud chatter from the patio. He and Emma both went into the screened-in porch while Lydia and the troops clamored inside.

He heard Penny's voice, higher than it usually was. "Mom, you should never have gone after it."

Pippa ran to Emma and wrapped her arms around Emma's legs. "He ran away, Emma. He ran away."

Feeling empathy for all three daughters, Daniel looked at his oldest child, who had been quiet through all of this. With a shrug, Paris added, "Mom scared him, and I think she did it on purpose."

Obviously hoping to defuse the situation, Emma suggested, "Why don't you all get a snack. There are cookies in the cookie jar."

Penny and Pippa hurried into the kitchen and went to the cookie container while Paris trailed behind them.

Letting out a breath, Daniel studied his ex-wife, wanting to get her side of the situation. "What happened out there, Lydia?"

"They're all upset with me."

Patience weighed down Daniel's voice. "Can you tell me why?"

"We saw the dog."

"And?" he prompted.

"And it looked like it was going to come toward Pippa. He's scruffy and dirty and who knows what diseases he might carry. I shooed him away."

"You shooed him away from the girls." Daniel wanted to make sure he'd heard Lydia clearly.

"I did it for their own good, even if they can't see that."

He tried to tap his anger down into irritation. "Maybe

you need to see *their* point of view. For the past week they've set out food and water every night hoping to help this dog. The idea was that we would trap him, but this pup seems to be able to outsmart us. He waits until we've turned in to eat. I'd still like to catch him and take him to Furever Paws. Do you remember the animal shelter?"

Lydia nodded. "What can the shelter do?"

"It's a no-kill shelter. They will bathe him, examine him, make sure he's adoptable. Eventually, they'll find him a foster home until they can find him a permanent home. Just as Fiesta has found a home here, the three P's want him to find a home, too." He couldn't help the stern edge that came into his voice. "All three of our daughters are compassionate, Lydia. And the compassionate thing wasn't to shoo that dog back into the woods. I'm going to have to go out there and look for him just to make them feel better."

When Lydia's lower lip began to tremble, Daniel knew he was in for a rough time.

Tears filled her eyes.

He could only say, "Aww, Lydia, don't cry." Then she was in his arms whether he wanted her to be there or not. As he glanced over Lydia's head to Emma, he saw the hurt and disappointed expression on Emma's face.

He patted Lydia on the back, as he would have done with one of his daughters, and disentangled himself from her arms. "Why don't you go inside and have a glass of milk and cookies with the girls. Let them know you care about the dog, too. Tell them Emma and I have gone out to search for him."

"You and Emma?" Lydia asked.

"Yes. We'll take flashlights. Emma's not afraid to trek into the woods."

Lydia swiped her tears from her cheeks and fluffed her hair, as if having it in perfect place would help her relate to her daughters.

He wasn't sure what would wake up Lydia to some kind of understanding as to what worked and what didn't work with the three P's. But something had to or she would never bond with them again.

Once more, Daniel checked Emma's expression. It appeared to say she'd rather stay in the house with Lydia and his daughters than go out looking for the dog with *him*. He suspected it was the *with him* that was bothering her. She had every right to be upset at watching him console Lydia after what they'd shared.

He crossed to a corner of the sunroom, picked up two Maglites then gently cupped her elbow. "Come on, let's look. Maybe he didn't go too far."

After taking one last look at the kitchen, she followed him outside.

"Lydia's having a hard time," Daniel said. Even to his own ears, that sounded like defense of his ex.

"I know she is." Emma switched on her flashlight as they marched forward. "She's not using her motherly instincts. She's following an unwritten creed that she's developed because she thinks it will work. Just dropping back into their lives was jolt enough for them."

"I know that, and you know that, but she doesn't seem to be getting it."

"Maybe she doesn't *want* to get it, Daniel. Maybe this is just some last-ditch effort to find a different life rather than deal with the one she has. When she gets unhappy, she moves on."

"That's harsh, Emma."

"But it doesn't mean it isn't true."

They were at the edge of the woods now and Daniel shone his flashlight all around, as deep into the trees as he could. He thought about what Emma had said. Lydia was used to getting her own way. She'd been flirty and feminine and passionate and fun when he'd met her. They'd thought the honeymoon would last forever. However, children made a difference. Lydia had given him three lovely daughters, and he'd loved her for that. Maybe that had eclipsed everything else— her restlessness, her search for the next shiny new toy she could pay for from her trust fund. It was as if *he'd* never been enough.

After she'd left, he'd realized their marriage had ended soon after Penny had been born. Maybe it was the responsibility that had gotten to her. Maybe he hadn't done his share. But he'd been figuring out how to support them and maintain this beautiful house before her trust fund ran out. He'd had to take up the slack. At least, that's what he'd believed he was doing.

Emma started on the path that zigzagged through the woods. She wasn't afraid to choose her own path. She didn't seem to be afraid of the darkness or the thorns or anything else that stood in her way.

He remembered his cuts and scratches. Catching her shoulder, he ordered, "Wait."

"If we wait too long, he really will be gone."

"I don't think so. My guess is he has a nice little cave somewhere that he uses for shelter. The food on the porch has been gone every day so he's been eating and probably drinking. My guess is he'll eventually come out of hiding when he isn't scared. Going too far into the woods won't find him—and it might end in you getting hurt. I don't want you to suffer the same wounds I did."

She went perfectly still. "Are we still talking about the brambles in the woods?"

Emma's intuition always impressed him. Clasping her shoulder, he admitted, "I want to protect you from any kind of hurt."

"Sometimes that isn't possible."

He wrapped his arm around her shoulders and turned her back toward the house. "Do you want to talk about the hug I gave Lydia?"

"No." Emma's voice held a note of determination that he didn't like. If they didn't talk, he wouldn't know what thoughts were floating through her head. If they didn't talk, he couldn't tell her that his feelings for her were growing deeper.

On the other hand, if he did say it, he didn't know if she'd believe him.

The following evening, Emma left Paris in her room to pack up the supplies she'd need for her swim meet. Emma couldn't stop thinking about her day at work with Daniel while Lydia had chauffeured her daughters. There had been tension between her and Daniel even though they'd worked in separate spaces. She could feel the conflict and knew he could, too. What they were going to do about it, she didn't know. Their excursion outside last night to look for the dog hadn't made the situation any better.

Penny peeked out from Fiesta's room. "Nacho is scooting to the edge of the bin. Come see."

Perhaps kitten excitement was exactly what she needed...and the girls did, too.

Pippa was sitting in front of the box, watching them. That was unusual because she was usually walking all around, looking at the kittens from every angle and petting Fiesta.

As soon as Emma dropped to the floor, Penny pointed to the little yellow tabby. "Look at him move. Can he crawl out?"

"Not yet. It will be a little while until he can manage that. But he'll start scrambling around even more. And after their eyes open, they'll start learning to focus. Once they can do that and their muscles grow stronger, they'll outgrow this bin."

"Then we can let them in the rest of the house," Penny decided.

"I'm sure your father will have something to say about that."

"And Mom, too," Penny said dejectedly.

Emma tried to remain positive. "She's excited about Paris's swim meet tonight. Don't you think it will be fun with all of us going there to cheer on your sister?"

"You know what, Emma?" Penny asked.

"What?"

"I'm not glad Mom is back."

"Penny…"

"I'm *not*. She messed up everything. We were having a good time with you and—"

Suddenly Emma realized that Pippa was crying. Tears were running down her face and she hiccupped. Immediately Emma moved toward her and took her into her arms and onto her lap. "Hey, honey. What's wrong?"

But Pippa just shook her head.

"Are you upset by what Penny said? I'm sure she didn't mean it. Your mom being here is a special visit."

Pippa was still shaking her head, and Emma didn't know what that meant.

Emma said, "Penny, why don't you go see if Paris is ready. I have the feeling your mom and dad are ready to go."

"All right. But I did mean what I said." After a last look at her sister and Emma, she left the room and shut the door.

Emma turned her focus to Pippa again.

Pippa slipped her arms around Emma's neck and held on tight. Emma gently rocked her until the seven-year-old stopped crying. "Won't you tell me what's wrong?"

Pippa stayed silent. Then she whispered to Emma, "Mom doesn't really like us, does she?"

"Your mother *loves* you. Are you still thinking about the dog? Your mom's just not used to having animals around her. She knows now how important that dog is to you. If he comes around, she won't shoo him away again. I know one of these days we'll actually *see* him eating the food."

Pippa leaned away and looked up at Emma. "You really think so?"

"I do. And I also think you can look forward to this swim meet tonight. Wouldn't it be exciting if Paris has the best time?"

Pippa shrugged. "I guess so. Will you sit beside me?"

"I'm sure I can arrange that. But if your mom reads you a story tonight before you go to bed, I want you to listen closely. You won't just hear words, you'll hear the love in her voice."

"Really?"

Emma was going to hope and pray that when Lydia put Pippa to bed tonight, she'd give her extra affection. She'd have to say something to Lydia. Maybe this time Daniel's ex-wife would listen.

* * *

Daniel sat on the bleacher, Emma beside him, Pippa beside her, then Penny, then Lydia. Lydia kept glancing his way, and he wasn't sure what that was about. He did know that there seemed to be a wall up between him and Emma—a wall that he wanted to tear down. He wasn't sure if she wanted the same thing. He couldn't blame her for being upset. His daughters needed her, but she was trying to let Lydia find her place with them. On top of that, *he* needed her. However, she didn't seem to believe that. He had to figure out a way to show her.

Penny leaned toward him and pointed to the pool. "Paris is up next as soon as the whistle goes off."

Beside her, Lydia put her hand on Penny's shoulder. "Don't yell. Your dad knows."

Don't yell? Daniel just shook his head. Everybody was yelling and cheering and calling out. This wasn't a sit-down dinner, for heaven's sake.

When he looked down the row, he saw that Pippa had leaned against Emma, and Emma had encircled her with her arm. What was going on there? He noticed Pippa had been quieter than usual lately. That could be because of Lydia, or it could be something else. He'd have to talk to Emma about it after they got out of here.

His shoulder brushed against Emma's. She moved away and he thought again that he had to do something quickly or he was going to lose her.

Nevertheless, for right now, his attention had to be on Paris. He knew she was a good swimmer. Especially tonight, she'd told him she wanted him to pay close attention. She wanted to break a team record because she was competitive clear through. That could be good but it could also make her concentrate too much on winning.

As soon as the whistle went off, Daniel stood to cheer. Emma did, too, and so did Pippa and Penny. Lydia gave them all a puzzled look.

After a few moments of hesitation, she stood and yelled, "Go, Paris."

Daniel smiled. Maybe she was catching on.

Paris was ahead of her competitors, swimming powerfully for a girl her age. When she reached the other end of the pool, she turned around and started back. She was still about an arm's length ahead of her closest rival. She was giving this swim all the power she could. When she reached the wall, the coach kneeled at her lane and blew his whistle. As she stood in the water, he lifted her hand and she pumped the air. Her time was posted on the scoreboard. She had beaten last year's record.

"Let's go congratulate her," Daniel suggested.

They all went trooping down the bleachers and over to Paris's lane. She'd hoisted herself out of the water and stood. But as soon as she did, her body swayed like a reed in the wind.

Daniel ran to her and caught her before she fell. He murmured to her, "Just sit here. I'll have somebody check you out."

"No, Dad."

This time he wasn't listening to her. The medic who serviced the swim team came running over. Daniel stepped back to let him do his job. After he thoroughly checked out Paris, he said, "Her pulse is fast, but I think the adrenaline rush of putting out all that energy suddenly stopped and she crashed."

Daniel said to Lydia, "Why don't you take Pippa and Penny and go home. Emma, will you stay with Paris while she gets changed and make sure she's okay?"

Their gazes met. There was no wall between them when Emma answered, "Of course, I will."

Lydia had her arm around Pippa. "Come on, honey. We'll see your dad and Paris when we get home."

Daniel knew Lydia had forgotten Emma on purpose. He'd deal with that later.

Daniel could see Emma was watching Paris carefully as she followed his daughter into the women's locker room. Crossing to the exit door, he pushed through it.

There was a bench in the hallway, and he sat, ruminating about the whole situation. When Emma and Paris emerged from the locker room, Emma said, "Let's sit over there and talk for a few minutes."

Paris glared at her, but Emma didn't seem to care.

"I think I know why Paris almost fainted," Emma said. "Paris, tell your dad what you had to eat today."

Paris mumbled, "Orange juice and a piece of toast for breakfast, and a salad for lunch."

Emma said, "I'm going to walk outside so you two can talk."

Daniel was so pleased Emma was as perceptive as she was.

Paris wouldn't look at him.

"Emma talked to you about the nutrition you need for your body, didn't she?"

"She talked about Fiesta," Paris mumbled.

"But you knew she was also talking about you."

"I guess." She looked down at her hands in her lap.

"Paris—" He put his arm around her shoulder. "Will you tell me why it's so important to you to be thin. Is it because of bullying at school, other girls…?"

"No, nothing like that."

"Then what is it, honey?"

He saw his daughter's eyes become moist. "I want to look like Mom. But to do that, I have to diet like she did. I can remember. And she exercised every day. She still does. She has weights in her room. She brought them in her suitcase. And, Dad, isn't that what I have to do to be pretty and get a boyfriend?"

Daniel didn't even want to think about Paris dating, but he knew the time would be coming quicker than he expected. "Tell me something. When we walked in here tonight, at least three boys said hello and wished you good luck. Do you remember that?"

"That was Tommy, Brent and Casey. They run track. I watch their practices sometimes and cheer them on."

"They seemed to like you. Boys will like you for your inner qualities as well as your looks. You're beautiful inside and out, Paris."

"You're not objective!" she protested.

"The boys watching you at that swim meet were plenty objective."

Paris's eyes seemed to light up. "Really?"

"Yes, really. You can't swim like that without the nutrition to power you. What if you had felt weak in the middle of that heat?"

"That *would* have been dangerous, I guess."

"It definitely would have been dangerous."

Emma had come back into the school and raised her eyebrows in question.

Daniel nodded for her to join them. When she reached the bench, he said, "Paris is going to eat more so that she stays strong and can swim her heart out if she wants."

Emma crouched down and looked Paris in the eyes. "I'll help you modify a meal plan. It will be healthy and keep you at an appropriate weight for your height and age. We can ask your mom to help."

"Do you diet?" Paris asked Emma.

"No, I don't. I just try to eat good food in the proper proportions. That has seemed to work for me."

Daniel stood. "On the way home, we're going to stop and get Paris a milkshake. Healthy enough for you?" He grinned.

"It will be a start in teaching her about carbs and calories," Emma responded wryly.

But then she smiled back at him and he thought maybe they could return to a good place again. He just had the best idea to get them there.

Chapter Thirteen

The next morning, after Emma and Paris checked on Fiesta and her kittens, Emma was pleased to see Paris wanted to help her make breakfast. The night before she and Paris had gone over what a good diet would contain and Emma had made her a healthy meal, to help her get a better grounding before starting her day at camp. She'd also said she'd eat something in the boxed lunch the camp provided, even if it was peanut butter on one piece of bread.

That was progress.

Since Emma had spent most of the evening with Paris last night, she hadn't talked to Daniel. He, Lydia, Pippa and Penny had watched a movie. Paris had insisted it was too childish for her.

But before Emma turned in, she'd noticed Lydia and Penny talking. That, too, was progress and she'd left the

Sutton family alone to connect. But when she'd gone back to her room, she'd felt sad.

Today, after she dropped the three P's off at camp, she went to Daniel's office. She'd been hopeful when Lydia had said she'd pick up the girls after their camp and take them shopping.

That was exactly what Lydia was here for—time with her daughters. Emma could spend the whole day working with Daniel if he needed her.

However, after she parked and used the back door to go inside, she found Megan was out of the office at the courthouse and Raina Clark was back from Arkansas!

As she'd thought on first meeting Raina, Emma was struck again by how attractive Daniel's office manager was. She was probably in her early- to mid-thirties. Why hadn't anything developed between Daniel and Raina in the two years since his divorce? Daniel had told her he hadn't dated since Lydia left. Maybe he'd been so hurt he'd simply looked at Raina as an employee and nothing more.

Raina smiled. "Hi, Emma."

"You're back," Emma said lamely as her glance went to Daniel.

He shrugged. "I didn't know she was returning."

"My bad," Raina said. "I only got in last night, but I didn't notify Daniel because I'm not staying."

"You're giving up your job here?" Emma asked, mystified.

"I've asked Daniel for a leave of absence. My parents and my sister need me in Arkansas. My parents have chosen a retirement community but they're going to need help moving and getting settled, and I'd like to spend time with them while I can."

As Daniel studied Emma to see how she'd taken that news, he said, "That means I'll need you to stay on as my office manager. How does that sound?"

Emma wasn't sure how that sounded. Yes, she still needed the job, but she didn't want him to need her simply for that.

She remembered how he and his family had looked last night as they'd eaten popcorn that Lydia had popped and laughed at the movie. She was definitely beginning to feel like the proverbial third wheel. She'd have to make a decision soon on what she was going to do about that.

After Raina hugged Daniel goodbye and left, he crossed to Emma. Today he was dressed in a cream oxford shirt with the sleeves rolled up, khaki pants and docksiders. She liked the fact that he towered above her. It made her feel feminine. She liked the fact that he could sweep her up into his arms. She also liked the fact that he was a toucher, and each of his touches meant something special to her.

Now his green eyes were dark and deep as he gently held her by the shoulders. She could feel the heat of his hands, of each finger, through her summer top. She'd worn mint-green slacks with a yellow blouse along with white sandals. He was scanning her now as if he wanted to swallow her whole.

A shiver rippled up her spine and her body tingled from the memories of what they'd shared, along with the anticipation of what they could share now.

"The job is definitely yours if you want it."

She wanted to jump on the offer and say, "Of course I'll take it," but the situation made her hesitate. "Can you let me think about it for a couple of days?"

She could see that her answer surprised him, but he

rallied. "Of course, take as long as you need. I know it's a lot doing this and being a nanny to the three P's."

She wanted to tell him that that wasn't it at all, but she truly wasn't sure he'd understand where she was coming from.

"I spoke to Lydia last night," he said.

"About what?" Emma asked.

"About spending more time with the three P's. If that's why she's here, then that's what she should do. That's why she said she'd take them shopping today. That's something she loves to do, so hopefully the girls will have a good time."

"I hope so, too, though Pippa tires out quickly and Paris is disappointed if a dress she wants doesn't fit. Then there's Penny, who only wants to look at jeans."

Daniel chuckled. "Yes, well, Lydia will learn their likes and dislikes. Before we get to work, there was something else I wanted to tell you."

"What?"

He ran his hand up her neck and fingered one of her curls. "I have a surprise for you tomorrow. We're both taking the day off. Around midmorning, you and I are going on a little road trip."

"Where are we going?"

"That's the surprise, so don't ask any more questions. I won't answer them."

The lightness in Daniel's tone buoyed her own spirits. Time alone with him. That could be just what they needed. She was looking forward to tomorrow already.

Emma had decided to make braised pork chops with pineapple, parsleyed potatoes and carrots with an orange-juice glaze. After Daniel came home, he set his messenger bag on one of the chairs and came over to Emma. When his arm ringed her waist, she looked up from the glaze she was making.

She felt his heat right away, took in the lime scent of his cologne. His shoulders were broad and she felt his presence from her bangs to her espadrilles.

"Cooking a major supper tonight?" His mouth was very close to her ear as his breath fanned a curl.

All she wanted to do was wrap her arms around him. Instead she responded, "The girls will be hungry. Shopping takes a lot of energy, you know."

He kissed her neck. It was just a little nibble, and yet she felt her toes curl. "I don't know. I do it as little as possible."

"You said Lydia likes to shop. Don't be surprised if each of them is carrying four bags or more."

Now he brushed aside her hair and kissed the nape of her neck.

She let out a long breath. "You're distracting me."

"That's my intent. It looks to me as if that glaze is done. Maybe you could just turn it down to warm...at least for a couple of minutes."

She'd gone beyond warm the minute he'd stepped into the kitchen. She switched the burner to low as he'd suggested and turned to face him. As soon as she did, he slid his hand under her curls and kissed her with a need that she suspected had been building since last night. She knew that because hers was building, too.

They kissed once, twice, three times and then he stepped away.

"That was a very nice distraction," she said with a smile, her words slow and shaky.

Before he could respond, they both heard the car in the driveway. Daniel dropped his hands and stepped away.

Emma hardly registered the fact that they were acting as if they were doing something wrong. But with Lydia and the three P's piling through the kitchen door, she kept silent.

As she suspected, she counted several bags. But when she turned her gaze to Pippa, she only saw her carrying one.

Pumping enthusiasm into her voice, she asked, "How was the shopping trip?"

"Fabulous," Lydia said. "And just look at our nails. Come on, girls, show Emma and your dad."

Even Pippa had nails painted with glitter and half moons with bright colors.

"You'll have to show me what you found," Emma told them all. "Maybe you could have a fashion show for your dad." She assumed that was something Lydia could be enthusiastic about.

"Oh, no," Paris said, sidling up to Emma. "He won't like what I bought. My tummy shows."

Emma knew that was the style but Paris was right. Daniel wasn't going to like it.

Penny wrinkled her nose. "No fashion show here. I've just got shorts and tops. Dad knows what they look like. I wear them for soccer all the time. I know soccer's over now, but Mom said I could wear them in the fall. I didn't want any of the dresses she showed me."

"Not even one dress?" Daniel teased.

Penny merely responded, "Come on, Dad."

To Emma's surprise, Pippa said nothing.

Paris said, "I'm gonna go watch the kittens." Penny seconded her and followed behind.

Daniel grabbed his messenger bag. "I'll be in my office until supper. There are a few phone calls I didn't get a chance to make at the office." He gave Emma a smile that easily said he'd like to kiss her again. Instead, he walked down the hall.

Emma wrapped her arm around Pippa. "Why don't you tell me what you bought?"

But Pippa took one look at Emma and ran down the hall after her dad.

Turning to Lydia for an explanation, she found Daniel's ex-wife looking through the bags. But she looked up when she felt Emma's gaze on her. "I was looking for something I bought for Pippa. It was a cute necklace with a little dog hanging on it. She said she didn't want it, though, and I couldn't understand why. She was so quiet after I picked them up from camp. She's not usually like that, is she? Is she moody?"

Lydia apparently was trying to get to know her daughters by picking up on their personality traits and that was a positive step. "Daniel told me that after you left, Pippa had bad nightmares every night and cried herself to sleep. She's not usually a quiet child. She has a lot of excitement and enthusiasm. My guess is she's afraid you're going to leave again."

"I don't know what I'm going to do," Lydia admitted.

Suddenly from down the hall, Daniel called, "Emma, can you come here a minute?"

Emma turned to the potatoes that were slowly simmering on the stove and the glaze that she'd turned down on low.

Lydia motioned toward Daniel's office. "Go ahead, I'll keep an eye on this."

Whether she could trust Lydia to do that or not, Emma didn't know for sure. She did know that Daniel needed her in his office and she hurried that way. When she got there, she saw he was sitting in his desk chair holding

Pippa in his arms. She was sobbing. Over his daughter's head, he told Emma, "Close the door."

Unable to imagine what was wrong, Emma gently shut the door. She went to Daniel and Pippa and perched on the corner of the desk. "What's the matter?"

Daniel lifted Pippa's chin with his thumb. "Tell Emma what you told me. You know you have to."

With a hiccup, Pippa confessed, "I took your locket. It's in my room in my sock drawer." She could hardly speak because she was still crying.

Although Emma was glad to know the locket was safe, she was more concerned about this little girl. "Why did you take it, honey?"

"Because I didn't think you'd leave without the locket. I heard you tell Dad you were thinking about leaving. I don't want you to leave."

Emma crouched down in front of Pippa, not knowing what to tell her. She took the little girl's hands in hers.

Seeing that she was at a loss, Daniel explained, "Pippa, I want you to get to know your mom while you have the chance. I don't know if she's going to stay. I don't think *she* knows if she's going to stay. And Emma can't make promises about leaving that she can't keep."

Did that mean Daniel didn't trust her to stay? That if she made a promise she might not keep it…just as his ex-wife hadn't kept her marriage vows?

This situation was messy, so messy, and she didn't want to hurt these three precious girls.

"Come here, Pippa, and give me a hug," she said to the little girl.

When Pippa stopped crying and hugged Emma, Daniel suggested, "Why don't you take Emma with you and give her her locket."

Emma took a tissue from the nearby credenza and tenderly wiped the tears from Pippa's eyes.

"Do you still like me?" Pippa asked.

"Yes, I like you. I *more* than like you. Nothing's going to change that."

After she stood, she held out her hand to Pippa and Pippa took it. As they climbed the steps to the little girl's room, Emma wished she wasn't so confused about everything.

As Daniel drove to Raleigh with Emma, he hoped the surprise would be a winner. Emma hadn't spoken much on the way, and he hoped this afternoon would mend whatever was wrong between them. He knew he'd been letting Lydia take up too much of his time. That's what this afternoon was all about—time for him and Emma. The truth was…he was tired of thinking about the right thing or wrong thing to do. His love for Lydia had died a long, long time ago. On the other hand, he realized his daughters might need her in their lives.

He'd almost reached the hotel when Emma glanced at him and said, "Lydia didn't seem particularly overjoyed at spending the day with the girls. She did take them shopping yesterday. Maybe it was too much to ask."

"She's their mother, Emma. She should want to be with them, and that's all I'm going to say on the subject. Today is just about us."

Emma sent him a smile that looked hopeful. Her smile could light up a room. It certainly lit *him* up.

Emma seemed surprised when they turned into the parking lot of the hotel. He parked and she turned to him, looking puzzled. "Are we sightseeing today?" she asked lightly.

"Not exactly." He unfastened his seat belt and then unfastened hers. "Our sightseeing is going to consist of looking, touching and holding each other. What do you think?"

Slight lines creased her brow. "I guess we didn't bring a change of clothes because you didn't want Lydia to know."

"I just thought it was better all around if we were discreet. I think you'll like what I've set up for us. We can check in early and stay as late as we want, though I guess we should get back around dinner time." He hated putting a limit on their time together. But right now, it was necessary.

Emma felt a bit disconcerted as she scanned the lobby after she and Daniel walked inside the hotel. It was easy to see that the establishment had a classic elegance about it without being gaudy. The arrangement of flowers in a tall vase on a table in the foyer was brimming with lilies, spider mums, tulips and roses. They were bright and colorful. Emma felt a little embarrassed when they checked in without luggage. After all, everyone knew what that meant. But the staff was discreet and no one even quirked an eyebrow.

On the way up to their room in the elevator, Daniel took Emma's hand. She asked, "How did you pick this hotel?"

"One of my clients had stayed here. He told me about it. I remembered what he'd said."

A client who was getting a divorce or maybe a client who had had an affair?

They didn't see anyone else as they walked down the carpeted hall together. Daniel found their room and inserted the card key, and when the green light appeared, he opened the door.

They stepped inside to a beautifully appointed room. As they passed a wet bar, Emma peered into the bathroom and spotted a tub with multiple jets.

Daniel encircled her with his arms and grinned. "This is going to be fun."

Emma couldn't help but catch his enthusiasm. She spotted the king-size bed, with its blue-and-white silky sheened coverlet and the pillows that were bigger than she'd ever seen. The sitting area, with a mahogany-finished sofa, love seat and chair, was ready for anyone who wanted to watch the TV there.

However, Daniel went to the huge dresser across the room and opened the armoire doors. Another, much larger flat-screen TV was hidden inside. When there was a knock on the door, Daniel went to answer it. Over his shoulder, he explained, "That's lunch. I didn't forget that breakfast was a long time ago."

"You arranged this beforehand?"

"I certainly did. Just wait until you see dessert. We can have it with the meal or we can wait and eat it later for a snack."

The hotel employee, dressed in a white shirt with black trim and black slacks, wheeled in a shelved cart.

Daniel instructed, "You can just set lunch on the table over by the window." He checked with Emma. "Is that okay with you?"

"That's fine." Eating lunch together at the table would seem more normal than checking into a hotel and jumping into bed. Not that she didn't want to jump into bed with Daniel. She did. But she didn't want to feel as if… as if this was just an affair.

As she watched the waiter set up lunch, the scent of the food wafted toward her. There was soup that looked as if it might be cream of broccoli, one of her favorites. A large Caesar salad was obviously for the two of them. There were at least three types of sandwiches—two huge burgers on sesame-seed buns with tomato and lettuce garnish, a sandwich with salad of some type, probably chicken, and a club sandwich with bacon, ham and turkey. Daniel had thought of everything.

Two covered dishes still sat on the cart. Daniel motioned to the coffee table in the sitting area. "Can you put those over there?"

After the waiter did that, Daniel signed the bill, tipped the waiter and watched as he left. "What are those mysterious dishes?" she asked.

He took her hand and pulled her over to the love seat in front of the coffee table. "Let's just take a peek before we eat lunch. I don't want the soup and burgers to get cold." As he removed the lid from the first dish, Emma glimpsed at two slices of chocolate cheesecake. When she took the lid off the other dish, she spotted the chocolate-covered strawberries.

He picked up one by the green stem and held it to her lips. "Want a taste?"

The sparkle of enjoyment in his eyes lit up a joy inside her, too. She took a bite then licked her lips.

Daniel took a bite from the same strawberry and laid the stem on the dish. Then he took her into his arms and kissed her. He tasted like chocolate and strawberries and the future.

After he broke the kiss, he just held her for a few minutes and she snuggled into his shoulder. He'd been right about needing this time together. She loved him. Maybe today she'd finally discover what he felt about her.

They moved to the table, which looked out over the

cityscape. As they began their soup course, they talked about anything and everything other than Lydia and the three P's. It was a delightful break from ordinary life as they discussed more about their childhoods, art they liked, places they wanted to visit. After they finished eating and kept up the conversation, she learned that Daniel's father had taught him how to fish, how to paddle a canoe, how to swim. His mom had worked as a paralegal and that's how he'd become interested in the law. She'd made Christmas the best celebration every year and colored eggs at Easter along with taking him to church. His father had been more laid-back and had made furniture as a hobby.

"I'd like to take you on the Blue Ridge Craft Trail sometime. I think you'd like it."

"All different crafters?"

"That's right. Everything from weaving to candle-making to furniture. The trail will take you into the mountains. No four-star hotels there, but very cute bed-and-breakfasts."

He pushed aside his plate. "We did that food justice." Standing, he came around to her side of the table. "Dessert now or later?"

When she stood, she knew what she wanted and imagined he wanted the same thing—to be held in each other's arms. As soon as Daniel's lips came down on hers, she knew this was true love. They needed this time together. If it was possible, she wanted to stand beside him and go to bed with him every day and every night for the rest of her life. She wanted to see the sun rise and the sun set while he was holding her in his arms.

After he broke the kiss, he came back for another kiss again and again. No talking was needed. His kisses emptied the room of air until she was dizzy. As they undressed each other, she forgot about time, his ex-wife and all the complications that now didn't seem to matter. As she rid Daniel of his shirt, sunlight skidded across his jaw. She touched it and then she kissed it.

Their clothes flew here and there. All they cared about was the heat of their skin, the vehemence of their desire, the sweetness of each fingerprint on their heart, each embrace that finally took them to the bed. After Daniel swept back the coverlet and the sheet, they tumbled into the bed, holding on to each other. Daniel had learned quickly what excited her and she had learned what excited him. She knew if she kissed right behind his ear, he'd groan. She did it once, twice, and then again.

Rolling her under him, he titillated her body until she was hot and excited in every nerve ending. Emma kept her eyes open when Daniel entered her. She wanted to see the emotion in his. His eyes became a darker green and revealed the deep emotions he felt at everything they were sharing. When he made her his, she reveled in the feelings…and not just the physical ones. Those were simply the manifestation of everything in her heart that wanted to embrace him forever.

When they were one, when they were climbing the mountain to climax, she couldn't help herself, and murmured, "Daniel, I love you."

Extreme pleasure shook them both until Emma forgot to listen to his response. However, as they lay side by side again in the afterglow, she was unsettled by the fact that he hadn't said he loved her, too.

Chapter Fourteen

Emma had just experienced the most wonderful afternoon. She had to hold on to that instead of what she wanted from Daniel...or even what she needed. She could live in this romantic pink glow for a while. It would hold her until she and Daniel were alone again... until she could tell him out loud and clearly what she felt. They chatted on the way home. Every now and then Daniel would reach over and take her hand and they would silently revel in what they'd experienced together. Thoughts of Lydia and the three P's didn't invade their intimacy until Daniel veered onto his street and then pulled into the driveway.

After he switched off the SUV, he unfastened his seat belt and then unfastened hers. Leaning toward her, he caressed her cheek. "One more kiss before we go inside."

She was afraid everything would change between

them when they went in. But it shouldn't. Not after what they'd just experienced together.

The tenderness in Daniel's kiss was obvious. With each nibble of her lips and each stroke of his tongue, he showed how much he cared. Closing her eyes, she was back in that hotel room with him, shutting out the world. Once they realized how long the kiss had gone on, they broke away from each other. They recognized reality when they felt it. She just hoped they were on the same page with everything else.

Emma and Daniel had hardly reached the front door when it was thrown open. The three P's poured out.

Pippa wasn't just crying, she was actually sobbing. She ran to Emma. "I want my hair back."

Emma took a good look at her and realized her pretty, wavy, shoulder-length hair had been trimmed into a pixie cut!

Lydia stood in the open doorway. "I took them all to a hair salon because I had an appointment I didn't want to break. Doesn't it look adorable?"

Through her hiccups, Pippa was shaking her head. Her hair didn't swing any more. "I *hate* it."

Daniel was scowling. He asked Lydia, "Didn't you ask her before you had it cut?"

"Why would I ask her? She's only seven. I know what looks best around her face. Plus, this won't take nearly as much care."

Emma felt annoyed with Lydia and sad for Pippa. Yes, the long hair had required maintenance, but she hadn't minded. She had brushed Pippa's hair and arranged it in pigtails and French braids. She'd liked doing it for her. Crouching down to Pippa without hesitation, she said softly, "I understand you don't like it, but it will grow out."

"By tomorrow?" Pippa wailed.

"Not by tomorrow. But you know what? I bet we could find some cute hair bands with butterflies or flowers on them. You could wear those in your hair. They'd look cute." Emma pretended to pinch Pippa's nose. "Especially with this button nose."

Pippa brushed Emma's hand away with a tiny bit of a smile. "My nose isn't a button."

Paris had her lips smashed together as if whatever was inside of her was bursting to come out. She pointed to Lydia. "She doesn't know how to handle kittens. She wouldn't even clean out their litter box. *I* did it."

"Those kittens are dirty. They can't even wash themselves yet," Lydia pointed out. She showed Daniel her arm. "That momma cat scratched me."

Now Penny chimed in. "That's because you dropped one of the kittens and Fiesta was protecting her baby."

Lydia threw up her hands. "Obviously I'm doing everything all wrong. None of you want me here. I'm going back to Virginia."

As she stalked away, Daniel went after her.

Emma knew exactly what she had to do. She couldn't separate a mother from her children. She'd lived without her mom all these years. She couldn't let the three P's lose their mom. And she couldn't help thinking that her being around was making the problems between Lydia and the girls worse—that Lydia was messing up because she felt threatened by Emma and the way the girls turned to her first. If Emma stayed, she was sure Lydia would leave...but would that be what was best for the three P's? She could stay and fight for Daniel, but who would lose? His daughters.

As soon as she settled down the three P's, she'd pack.

Daniel hurried after Lydia, wanting to stay with Emma and the three P's, yet knowing for his daughters' sake he couldn't let their mom leave their lives.

In the spare room, Lydia had pulled one of her suitcases onto the bed and was packing it. She'd already put in pairs of shoes. His guess was, one of the suitcases was devoted to them.

She glanced over her shoulder at him then went to the closet and plucked three handbags off a hook. She added those to the shoes.

"Lydia, you have to be more patient with Paris, Pippa and Penny. If you are, they'll be patient with you. Get their take on things. Ask their opinions."

Lydia brushed away his words with a fling of her arm. "I've made some decisions."

"Don't have a knee-jerk reaction to what just happened."

"This isn't knee-jerk, believe me. I've been thinking about it ever since I arrived. Don't you think I see the way Emma relates to them?"

Daniel knew Emma related like a mother should. Maybe not "should." Emma was Emma. She was filled with compassion. It was one of the many things he admired about her.

When she'd murmured to him that she loved him, Daniel hadn't been able to say it back. His life was so complicated. They hadn't known each other long. He couldn't make another wrong decision, for his daughters' sake.

He responded to Lydia. "Emma is just a naturally warm person."

"What you're saying is... I'm not."

"Don't put words in my mouth."

"And don't act as if we're still married. We're not. When I arrived here, maybe I had hoped there was still a slight chance for us. I've realized so many things over the past few days."

Daniel ran his hand up and down the back of his neck. He had to say what was true. "Lydia, our marriage had been over for a long time, even before we filed for divorce."

"I know, and I turned to Allen because we were more alike. I had a long talk with him last evening. He made me see I didn't try to make things better with you. I just ran away. The truth was, and is, I love the girls. But caring for them twenty-four hours a day..."

She shook her head. "That wasn't me then and it isn't me now. I do love Allen. And even though I came here looking for a solution instead of turning to him, he still loves me."

Daniel's view of Allen had been distorted ever since the affair. They'd been more than partners before that. They'd been friends. He knew he had to forgive Allen just as he'd forgiven Lydia or he couldn't move forward.

Trying to find out exactly what else was in Lydia's head, he said without judgment, "So you're going back to Alexandria and forgetting about the girls again?"

Her response was immediate. "No. I know I was wrong not to come back here and visit them. But I think I have to consider them and me differently."

"Differently?"

"As you've noticed, I'm not like Emma. I care about

shopping, hair and nails, the latest fashions. I don't care about soccer games and hiking in the woods and swimming tournaments. Now I know I'm going to have to become interested in those to connect with the girls. However, I think we'd be better off if they connect with me in my environment, too. Yes, I'll come back to Spring Forest to visit, but I'd like to show them the sights in Alexandria. Would you bring them there to visit me? I know you don't want to see Allen, but—"

"If Allen is part of your life, then if the girls visit you, he'll be a part of theirs, too, whether he's physically present or not, right?"

"You were always the practical one," Lydia murmured. "So you'll come and visit me with them, maybe with Emma, too?"

"That depends on Emma."

Lydia closed the suitcase on her shoes and purses. "No, Daniel, a lot of it is going to depend on you."

"I don't know what you mean."

"Sure you do. How she feels depends on whether she comes along as a nanny or as your significant other."

Tightness gripped his chest. "There's so much to consider."

Lydia shook her head. "No, there's not. My guess is that Emma is in her room packing to leave."

"What?" The word exploded from him.

"As you said, Emma is warm, compassionate and loving. I saw the look in her eyes down there when the girls turned to her instead of me. And I'm sure she saw my disappointment. She's the type of woman who will do what's best for Penny, Pippa and Paris. I suspect that she thinks she needs to leave so we can become a family again."

"She can't leave," Daniel said quickly.

"Why not, Daniel?"

The pieces of this puzzling dilemma slipped into place. Emma couldn't leave. Not because he needed her as a nanny or an office manager, but because he wanted her to be his life partner.

He loved her.

"You'd better go tell her, and you better make it good, or you're going to have an empty suite down there and a huge hole in your life."

After studying Lydia, Daniel asked, "What's the possibility that you and I can become friends?"

Lydia titled her head...and smiled. "It's a very good possibility."

"You're not going to leave tonight, are you?"

"I'll stay until morning. I do want to make sure that the three P's don't think it's their fault I'm leaving. Maybe I can show them a map of Alexandria on your computer, and we can discuss a visit."

"That sounds good," Daniel agreed. He turned toward the door. "I have to find Emma and tell her how I feel. I just hope she'll believe me."

As Daniel jogged down the stairs and headed for Emma's room, his heart had never beaten so fast. He should have analyzed his feelings and talked about their future before they left the hotel. He should have faced his feelings then. He just hoped it wasn't too late.

Emma hadn't even closed her door. The dresser drawers were pulled out, and her clothes lay straggled across the bed. The sight of her suitcase scared him like no other sight could.

He burst into Emma's suite. "You can't leave."

Tears ran down her cheeks and she turned to him. "Daniel, I have to leave. Paris and Pippa and Penny deserve to know Lydia. She deserves to know them. If I stay, I'll just be in the way."

"You are *not* in the way. I need you. My daughters need you."

Emma was shaking her head. "Ever since Lydia arrived, I've felt as if you turned to me on the rebound. I'm convenient, Daniel. And I don't want to be convenient. Your needing me is not a good enough reason for me to stay."

Daniel took Emma's elbow and guided her over to the bed to sit beside him. She kept her eyes on her lap, though.

"I need to catch you up on what's happening. Lydia had a long talk with her husband. They want to make their marriage work."

That statement coaxed Emma's face around to his.

He went on, "She's going back to Alexandria tomorrow morning. First, she's going to convince the three P's that they are *not* the reason she's leaving."

"She's leaving because of *me*," Emma said dejectedly.

"No, that's not true. She sees you as the loving woman you are, and she wants the girls to be in your care. She feels she has to learn how to relate to them on their terms, but also on her terms. She wants them and us to come visit her in Alexandria. I think she's right, Emma. Lydia is all about sightseeing, shopping and living someplace important. She considers Alexandria to be that and she wants to show it to her daughters. When she's on her own turf, I really do think she'll be able to relate to them better, and that they'll be more understanding toward her, too."

"She wants us to visit them?" Emma's dark brown eyes were wide with surprise.

"Yes. She can see how I feel about you, and I hope how you feel about me. I made a terrible mistake this afternoon, not telling you how I feel before we left the hotel."

He took both of her hands in his. "I love the way the right side of your lips turn up when you smile, your love of life, your compassion for anything furry with four feet. You give my daughters security they haven't known for a long time. But more than anything, you give me your desire, your understanding and, I hope, your love."

He stood and then kneeled on one knee before her.

Emma was crying and he hoped it was because she was happy, not because she was sad. He took her hand and gazed into her eyes. "I want you to be my partner, my confidante, my lover. But most of all, I want you to be my wife. Will you marry me, Emma Alvarez?" He held his breath waiting for her answer.

Emma felt as if she was on a merry-go-round that wouldn't stop spinning. She'd been so happy with Daniel this afternoon. But after they'd come home, she'd thought she should leave him for his own good. Now, gazing into his eyes, she couldn't believe he was asking her to be his wife. "Daniel, we haven't known each other long."

"I've known you long enough to know everything I need to know about you. I know you work hard. You have the biggest heart I've ever known, and you love with your body and soul. If you talk about need, that's what I need. How about you?"

She loved Daniel so much she felt as if her heart was going to burst. She leaned down to wrap her arms around his neck. "I love you, too, Daniel, more than I ever thought possible. Yes, I'll marry you."

Daniel stood and swept her up into his arms. As he kissed her, the intensity of it declared his promise to take care of her, stand beside her, be faithful to her and love her for the rest of his life.

After they ended the spectacularly long kiss, they broke away from each other. But Daniel couldn't stand the lack of contact. He leaned his forehead against hers. "We'll have to make sure that the three P's know they have two mothers instead of one."

"I promise I won't interfere whenever Lydia wants to spend time with them."

"We're going to make this work, sweetheart. I also realized I have to forgive Allen if he's going to be in Lydia's life…and my daughters' lives. This is going to be a process for all of us. We'll let the girls absorb all this slowly. I don't want them to think we're pushing them into relationships they don't want. What I'm sure of more than anything is that they'll turn to you on a daily basis. You have their hearts, Emma, just as you have mine."

Daniel could see in Emma's eyes that she felt the same joy he did—joy like he'd never known before. As he kissed her again, she held tight to him. He knew that they'd be holding on to each other for the rest of their lives.

Epilogue

A week later, Emma, Daniel and the girls walked into Furever Paws to volunteer. Lydia had left but she'd promised to call the three P's at least once a week. They could text or call her whenever they wanted. Daniel had already set up a visit to Alexandria for a few days in August before the girls returned to school.

The first person they encountered in the shelter was Rebekah. She handed each of them a paper with their assignment. When Emma reached out to take the sheet, Rebekah gave a little squeal at the engagement ring on Emma's finger.

Sunshine flowing through the windows caught the beautiful solitaire diamond. Daniel had surprised her with it last night.

"It's official," Emma said.

Daniel wrapped his arm around her. "More than official."

Pippa hugged Emma around the legs. "Emma's gonna stay with us forever."

Rebekah glanced at Penny and Paris, who were also smiling. "Best wishes to all of you," she said. She asked the girls, "Do you want to see the new cat enclosure? It's almost finished."

They all trailed after Rebekah to examine the expansion project. Emma quickly glanced at the screened-in porch where the cats could experience outside while still being safe inside.

"Are you going to add chairs to the porch?" Emma asked. "That way the cats can get used to people being around them, which would make them more adoptable."

Rebekah nodded. "We were going to build a few cat trees, but that's a great idea."

After examining every nook and cranny of the enclosure, Pippa and Paris went to play with the puppies. Penny stuck with Emma. They were going to give attention to the animals in quarantine.

"I know we have to wash our hands really good afterward," Penny said. Then she leaned close to Emma. "Did you talk to Dad about the kittens?"

"I did. Why don't you go over there and talk to him?" Emma was getting supplies ready to clean out cages.

Emma watched as Penny went to her dad. They had a conversation for at least five minutes. One of the other volunteers took Penny with her to give her instructions on how much food to pour into the dogs' bowls.

Daniel, with a booklet in hand, came over to Emma. "She asked me about the kittens," he said.

"And what did you say?"

"Since you all ganged up on me, and since those kittens are so dang cute, I did make a few calls this morning. Two of my clients have kids Penny's age. They've wanted pets for a long time. I told them these kittens would be socialized really well. They're coming over to take a look at them, maybe this weekend."

"And the others?" Emma asked.

He swung his arm around her. "I suppose if we can't find homes, we'll keep Fiesta and two kittens. You think that would make everyone happy?"

Even though they were standing at Furever Paws, even though people were milling about, Emma threw her arms around Daniel's neck and kissed him. She kept the kiss short but satisfying.

"To be continued later?" he asked. "Remember, I'm going to make an honest woman of you in July."

They had decided there was no reason to wait to get married. "I can hardly wait to be your wife."

"And I can hardly wait to be your husband. When I talked to your father last night, he seemed to like the idea of being a granddad to Paris, Penny and Pippa. I told him within the next few years, he may have another grandchild. What do you think?"

"I think it's a wonderful idea." Emma knew she and Daniel would have obstacles and challenges to contend with, but they would handle them...together.

As they gazed into each other's eyes, Daniel kissed her again, reminding her that true love was the greatest joy of all.

* * * * *

MILLS & BOON

Coming next month

FROM HEIRESS TO MUM
Therese Beharrie

'Still can't get used to this view,' Hunter said quietly as she stopped next to him.

Autumn followed his gaze onto the city of Cape Town. When she'd moved out of her family home—the Bishop mansion, as some people liked to call it—she hadn't tried to find somewhere outside the city she'd grown up in to live. She'd merely been drawn to the Bouw Estate.

It had green fields that exploded with wildflowers; rolling hills beyond the fields; a river that surrounded the estate. The old manor and barn on the property had been renovated into what were now her home and her bakery, respectively.

'You didn't come here at eleven at night to talk about this view.'

His eyes slid over to her, the brown of them a well of emotion, before his head dipped in a curt nod. 'You're right.'

She gestured to the outdoor table she'd lovingly selected when she'd furnished her house. 'Shall we?'

He nodded, pulled a chair out and stepped back. With a sigh, she sat down, thanking him when he pushed it back in. She waited as he sat down opposite her. A long silence followed. She used it to study him. To watch the emotions play over his face.

When his eyes met hers, she caught her breath, and wished she had something to drink to distract herself from how vulnerable all of this made her feel.

'I don't know how to say this,' he admitted eventually.

She let air into her lungs slowly. 'Just...get it out.'

He angled his head, as if accepting her suggestion, but didn't speak.

'Hunter.' She paused. 'Are you in trouble?'

He opened his mouth, and Autumn could almost see his lips forming no, but then he closed it again. Rubbed a hand over his face; took a deep breath.

'I am.'

She straightened. 'Yeah? You're in trouble?'

His eyes shone with an emotion she couldn't quite define. It disturbed her. She'd dated him for two years; they'd been friends for one more. She should be able to tell what he was feeling.

'Yes.'

After a brief moment of hesitation, she laid a hand on the one he'd rested on the table. 'What's going on?'

He took a breath, then exhaled sharply, his gaze lowering.

'I'm a father.'

Continue reading
FROM HEIRESS TO MUM
Therese Beharrie

Available next month
www.millsandboon.co.uk

COMING SOON!

We really hope you enjoyed reading this book. If you're looking for more romance, be sure to head to the shops when new books are available on

Thursday 2nd May